BOSTON BLUEY

BLUEY
Double Trouble

Also by Audrey & Clifford B. Bowyer

Boston Bluey
Boston Bluey: Double Trouble

BOSTON BLUEY

Daughter and Daddy Superheroes
Book 2

DOUBLE TROUBLE

by
Audrey & Clifford B. Bowyer

SILVER
LEAF
BOOKS

HOLLISTON, MASSACHUSETTS

BOSTON BLUEY: DOUBLE TROUBLE
Copyright © 2020 by Audrey & Clifford B. Bowyer

Cover Art by Vince Sunico;
Back Cover Coloring by Audrey Bowyer.

First printing March 2020
10 9 8 7 6 5 4 3 2 1

ISBN (hardcover) # 978-1-60975-259-0
ISBN (paperback) # 978-1-60975-260-6
ISBN (eBook) # 978-1-60975-261-3
LCCN # 2020933223

Silver Leaf Books, LLC
P.O. Box 6460
Holliston, MA 01746
+1-888-823-6450

Visit our web site at www.SilverLeafBooks.com

For the most loving, caring, and supportive Grandmother and Mother in the world. Throughout all of your own battles and struggles, much like a superhero, you always persevere and keep focusing on what is important to you...

Like the smile and affection of your Granddaughter!

We love you Grandma!

BOSTON BLUEY

BLUEY

Double Trouble

CHAPTER

1

"Unfortunate. Unfortunate when our community's children are put in danger and over three hundred guests on a night of celebration turned tragic. But it is not all bad, as this reporter has learned, there was something, someone, who helped in all of this chaos. With the Emergency Exit blocked, the fire spreading quickly, the theatre at capacity, and the performers separated from their loved ones, it would be easy to see how tragic this night could have gone. I am reminded of night club tragedies, where only a handful of souls are fortunate enough to be survivors. But that was not the case here.

"Here, many people were witness to something else," reporter Evie Berman said as the image shifted from her to survivors of the dance recital fire.

"She was flying. Like, flying by the roof, and kept shouting for me to get my family out."

"I was trapped, and she swooped down from the sky and showed me a way past the flames. I wouldn't be here if not for that masked girl."

The little boy watching the news on the television stared at the people talking in awe. Was there really a little girl who saved the day? A little girl who could fly? A real life superhero? Right here in Bellingham? It was a dream come true!

The television changed channels, a band on the screen singing.

"Hey!" the little boy said, turning around to see his sister with the remote. "I was watching that!"

"Not anymore."

"I was here first!" he screamed.

"I'm older. Live with it," she replied as she got herself comfortable in the chair.

"Only by a few minutes!" he shouted.

"Still older," she smugly replied.

"I'll tell Mom."

"Good luck with that," the girl said, laughing off the

threat.

"Signah, please," the little boy pleaded. "It's only a news broadcast. It'll be over in a moment. I don't want to miss it."

The little girl stared at her brother, seeing his brown eyes beginning to well up. She snorted derisively, but switched the channel back so he could watch the end of the report.

The broadcast was still on. The little boy sat back down, absorbing every word. "She looked like she was my age," a little girl who was in the recital said. Then after a pause. "I wish *I* could fly!"

"Me too," the little boy said.

"*I wish I could fly,*" Signah said mockingly. "Puh-lease."

The screen then shifted back to the reporter. "Bizarre? Extraordinary? Reports have been coming in for weeks that there were genuine heroes in the area helping people out and asking for nothing in return. This reporter would be so bold as to change hero, to superhero. They are not just something out of a movie or comic book anymore. At least, not according to the survivors of this incident. You can be assured, we'll be closely monitoring and seeking more news and insight on this superhero duo, this Boston Bluey and Little Bluey. But for tonight, there is a theatre full of souls just grateful that these superheroes were here. This is Evie

Berman, WTB TV, back to you, Greg."

"Little Bluey," the little boy whispered, repeating the name.

Signah changed the channel when the broadcast shifted away from the story about the superheroes. "Happy now?"

"There's a real live superhero," the little boy said.

"Sign, you'd believe anything," Sighah said, laughing.

"You heard the people on the news. A little girl who could fly. It's real, I tell you, real!"

Signah twisted the crystal necklace around her neck back and forth several times, then said, "Just like my crystal gives me magical powers. Powers strong enough to curse you if you're not careful."

"Signah!" Sign said, looking frightened.

Signah just laughed. "You'd believe anything."

"She's real. You'll see. Right here in town. We'll hear about her again. Maybe even see her. Maybe... maybe..."

"Maybe what? She'll let you be her sidekick or something?" Signah said, laughing again. "Oh Sign, don't be so gullible." She began twirling her crystal again. "If she is real, it's not a sidekick or a fan she needs, but a villain who knows how to stop her."

Sign stared at his sister in shock. "You would want to be a villain," he finally said, his words bold as he grew angry with his sister. "If you were, I'd help her. I'd help her stop

12

you!"

She just laughed again. "Ooh, I'm so scared." She clutched her crystal tight and began waggling her fingers at him, chanting to herself.

Sign screamed and ran from the room, shouting for their mother.

Signah rolled her eyes and sighed. "Works every time." She then forgot all about taunting her brother and the reports of a flying girl as she watched the singer on the television rock the stage.

CHAPTER

2

"Nanny, scan please."

The hovering sentient metallic orb, Nanny, rose into the air and flew over to where Ally was working. As instructed, Nanny scanned what she was working on and concluded, "Your construction of the bow has been very effective. Composed of fiberglass-based composite materials capable of taking high tensile and compressive forces. The limbs are designed to store all of the energy of the bow, with no energy stored in the drawstring, which will make shooting the bow easy even for you at your young age. I project arrow speed to be fired, as currently designed, to be between

300 and 400 feet per second."

Ally waited for Nanny to finish her assessment, and asked, "Does that mean I did a good job?"

Nanny's mechanical eyes studied the bow again, almost showing a sign of humor in its android gleam, and said, "I believe your father would say you did an amazing job."

Ally smiled at that. "I just have to finish decorating it."

Nanny shifted her gaze to Ally. "I see no need for aesthetic value. The bow is fully functional and ready for you to test it."

"Nanny, I can't use this as it is," Ally said as she shifted through her bin of paints. She pulled out metallic pink for the base, then a glittery purple to coat it. "It's going to be shiny and sparkly."

"Are you still keeping this from your father?" Nanny asked, already knowing the answer.

"It's a surprise," Ally said innocently.

"A surprise he'll approve of?" Nanny asked.

"My last name is Archer. Of course I need a bow," Ally reasoned.

"Your father does not have a bow," Nanny pointed out.

"Well, maybe after he sees mine he'll change his mind," Ally said.

"You know this is the kind of project your father likes to do with you," Nanny said.

Ally hesitated at that. They did like to do things together. From building toys to baking and cooking to painting rooms. He always had her involved and walked her through it, but was there to make sure she didn't get hurt. The only reason she was with Nanny and not her Daddy at the moment was because he was meeting with his partner Heidi Warrin and some investors for their new company, Archer Innovations, LLC. The holoprojecting watch technology that he was launching needed financial backers so that they would have more widespread production and distribution for the launch. Both he and Heidi were quite excited about it.

"It's a surprise," Ally said again, trying to sound confident.

Ally Lynn Archer and her Daddy were strangers to this land. They came from a world similar to this one but far more advanced technologically and where everyone had uncanny abilities. It was still a mystery how it all happened. They received a package and when they opened it, some kind of portal, or a rift through the multiverse, sent them— Ally, her Daddy, Nanny, and their pet dragon Loveaby— from the home they knew to here. That's when they met Heidi Warrin and saved her life. She took them in after that, knowing nothing about their background. With Nanny's help, identities and backgrounds were created, some money was generated, and just like that they had a new life here.

They bought a patch of land and built a house, bought a new car, and her Daddy started up two companies. The first was considered the big money maker in the partnership with Heidi, who was an MIT graduate working an hourly job and desperate for an opportunity to prove just what she could really do. The second company was a book publishing company, Shimendyn Books, launching her Daddy's books that he had written on their world as his occupation after she had been born. Before she was born he was a Protector, a member of law enforcement. But then when it was just the two of them, he gave that all up and became a stay at home Daddy and wrote novels about his exploits in the Protectorate. Nanny fortunately was able to download the manuscripts and use them for the launch of the first book, a blend of Science Fiction and Superhero themes to a new world that seemed to crave new material on both.

But, the most important thing about coming here, they had powers when nobody else did. This world did not need to fantasize about superheroes, they could have real live ones! Ally didn't know if her power set would continue to reveal itself as she got older, or if she would only have the power of flight, but she could fly! With Nanny and her

Daddy's help, she designed a costume and became Little Bluey.

Her Daddy on the other hand was super strong, and could jump over vast distances, and was hard to hurt, and when he really concentrated he could channel electricity through his veins. All of this made him a very capable Protector. But here, it made him an amazing superhero. He took a little more convincing though than she would have liked. Ally wanted to be a superhero right away, but he was afraid that they would be hurt, or that their secret identities would be compromised. Still, after a very public outing where Ally flew for the first time to get some balloons at Celebrate Holliston Day, her Daddy agreed to help her design costumes and if they were going to be superheroes, they would do it right. That meant a lot of training, a lot of practice, and a lot of preparing to help others and not get hurt themselves. That's when he became Boston Bluey.

Beyond flying, even though she was not even five years old yet, Ally had a propensity for creating things and figuring out how things worked. She had a toy bow from the Disney movie *Brave* and always hit her mark, the suction sticking perfectly every single time. Her Daddy would try to do it and the arrows rarely would stick, or even shoot very straight. In preparation for him being at his meeting, Ally assembled a list of things she would need to design a real bow that Little Bluey could use, and had Nanny order the parts so that when he was at his meeting she could try putting it all together.

She finished applying the paint and looked it over. "Poffit," she said.

"You mean perfect," Nanny corrected.

"No, this is poffit," Ally said. She then began painting the arrows, too. Everything had to be the same. After the arrows were done and the bow was fully dry, she had Nanny help her with the final modifications, using some of the advanced technology from their world to create holo-projecting targeting to help her with her aim.

"Honey, I'm home!"

Ally looked up, hearing her father calling her. She set the bow down and rushed up to greet him. "Daddy! Daddy! Daddy!" she shouted as she ran and jumped into his arms.

"I missed you so much," he said as he kissed her a dozen times all over her cheeks, forehead, and head.

"I missed you, too," she said.

"With any luck, that's our last meeting for a while," he said. "I think it went really well."

"Yay!" Ally said.

"So how has your day been? What have you and Nanny been up to?"

Ally couldn't wait, her lips creasing into a huge smile

and she excitedly said, "Daddy, Daddy, I have a surprise for you!"

"A surprise? For me?" he asked.

"Come see!" she said as he set her down and then she ran to the stairs and back down to the basement.

"Not too fast," he said.

"I won't," she replied. "Come on, come on, you have to see!"

He followed her down and saw she had an entire workspace set up with tools, paints, gadgets, a quiver full of arrows, and a shiny and glittery pink and purple bow. "What's all this?"

"You know how I shoot really good with my Merida bow?"

"Yup," he said.

"And how we are the Archer's?"

"MmHm," he said.

"I decided to make my own bow for Little Bluey," Ally added excitedly.

He walked over and pulled one of the arrows, touching the sharp point of the head. "You could get hurt with these. Or hurt someone else."

Ally's eyes lowered. "I'll be careful," she said, mumbling slightly.

"Maybe we can remove the arrow heads and put some

kind of cushioned pad. Knock someone back or out instead of something that could pierce skin."

Ally shook her head up and down. "That's a good idea."

"Can I see it?"

She handed him the bow. He looked it over, testing it for weight and balance. "It's light."

"Good for me to handle," Ally pointed out.

"Have you tried it yet?"

"I wanted to wait for you," Ally said.

"Let's see what it can do," he said. He grabbed a few boxes of books and lined them up on the wall, and then leaned a pillow from the outside furniture against it. "We can buy a new pillow. This will do until we can get you a real target."

"Okay," Ally said.

"Remember, pull back gently, aim, breathe, and release," he said.

Ally took an arrow, nocked it, and drew the bowstring back. As soon as she did, in her line of sight, a nearly transparent-blue imaging appeared with circles and angles. She used that to aim for her target, the blue image darkening as she was on target, and then with a release of breath, she let the arrow go. It soared past the bow and right into the cushion all the way to the feathers, the arrow smacking into the box of books.

21

"WooHoo!" her Daddy cheered. "Right on target. And deep. You made that yourself?"

"With Nanny's help," Ally said.

Nanny rose up between them. "I merely provided guidance as you would have done. She designed this all by herself."

"I think we may have discovered your second super power," her Daddy said, chuckling to himself. "My Ally is going to be a little inventor. I love you so much."

"I love you more," Ally said.

"I don't know about that," he said.

"I love you to the moon and back," Ally said.

"I love you throughout the multiverse and back," he said, smiling.

"I still love you more."

"Well okay. If you say so."

"I know it."

"But one day you'll know, when you have a little girl or boy of your own, you can take all of their love for you, double it, and then you'll be close to knowing how much your Daddy loves you."

"I still love you more."

He laughed. "Come on, let's practice some more."

CHAPTER

3

"Daddy, I'm awake."

Cary's eyes flickered open, forcing the sleep and dreams away. He glanced over at the clock. 6:09. "Are you sure? It's awfully early."

"I'm awake," Ally repeated.

"Well okay," Cary said. As he got himself up, he glanced at the pillow next to him and saw Loveaby, their pet dragon, still sound asleep. "Let's be quiet so we don't wake up Loveaby."

"Okay," Ally said, looking at her dragon fondly.

"Did you want to read or watch a movie or something?

Relax a bit?" Cary asked, noting pain in his lower back from an old injury when he was in the Protectorate that never quite healed right and always bothered him when he first got up in the morning.

Ally's eyes lit up. "A movie!" She then put her hands over her mouth and looked at Loveaby. "It was an accident."

"She's still sleeping. No harm done," Cary said reassuringly. "What movie would you like?"

Ally thought about it for a moment, then got off of the bed and scanned the DVDs on the shelves of the princess bookcase that was by the door. She selected one, Bolt, a Disney movie about a dog that thought he was a superhero but was really an actor. "I want to watch this one."

He looked at the movie and said, "Okay." Ally was really into superheroes at the moment, but also all things with dogs and puppies, so Bolt combined both of those for her. He then took it and put it into the DVD player.

DVDs were new to him. The technology here was very different from where they had come from. But he liked them, and they have been growing a collection practically since the day they had arrived. Even technology here was changing, with Blu-Ray discs, then 4K UHD, with each version increasing in resolution, clarity, and sound. Cary met some people who swore by the better resolution, but he thought the DVDs were fine and bought those unless there was no other choice—some movies or television shows only came out in Blu-Ray. The other big thing was streaming services, where you pay for a subscription and then get to watch whatever you want. But Cary preferred to have something substantial in his hands that he could look at, read about, and allow Ally to select from their collection. Besides, if they only had streaming services, what happens when the service provider decides to take something down? What if it was something that they loved? The DVD is theirs forever. Also, it seemed like there were more and more streaming services popping up, each with their own fees and structure. Do you get all of them? Do you pick just one? He'd stick with DVDs. It worked for he and Ally.

He waited for the DVD to load and then turned back to bed. Ally was laying where he normally slept. "Scooch over," he said as he went to get back in bed.

Ally moved over, careful not to go too far and wake up Loveaby. Cary got back in bed, trying to position himself just right so the back pain wasn't too bad, and then Ally snuggled into him, her head on his shoulder as the movie started.

They rarely watched an entire movie or read an entire book in the morning. But it was still a nice way to relax a bit and slowly start the day instead of just jumping up and diving into whatever the day's agenda would be.

Cary picked up his phone about half way through the movie and looked to see if there were any new messages. A few junk emails trying to get him to buy things or coupons to go shopping. Nothing that caught his eye. He then checked the weather. It was February 21ˢᵗ, a time of the year that Heidi often commented was usually full of snow and was freezing, but the app on his phone said it was going to be in the seventies.

"Want to go to the park today?" Cary asked. "Looks like a nice day out."

"Yay!" Ally shouted, ready to get up and turn the movie off as thoughts of the park raced through her mind.

"Let's have some breakfast first," Cary said. "Then we'll take our baths or showers, get ready, and get going."

"Okay," Ally replied.

"What are you in the mood for today? Pancakes? French Toast? Omelet?" Cary liked to give her some options when picking out food. He had always found that options were a good thing. Ally felt more involved in the decision making process, even if she was selecting from a limited number of choices, and she was far more likely to eat what he made for her. It worked quite well for them.

"Let me think about it," Ally said, stroking her chin as if in deep thought. "Pancakes!"

"Pancakes it is," Cary said. "Regular pancakes, Mickey Mouse pancakes, or dog bone pancakes?" It's been a while since she said Mickey Mouse ones, but for those he did simple pancakes with two smaller pancakes connected at the top to make mouse ears. The tricky part was flipping them without the ears breaking off. The dog bones were her latest craze, with a thin strip of pancake and little bumps at both sides of each end to look like a doggie-treat.

"Dog bone, please," Ally decided.

"Dog bone it is," Cary said.

They began to head downstairs, but Ally stopped and held her arms up. "Carry me."

"I'd be delighted," Cary said as he picked her up and continued on down the stairs. They went into the kitchen and he set her down on the counter. He then began with their morning vitamins and poured each of them a glass of orange juice. He set the orange juice down next to her and held his palm out with four vitamins in it. "Which ones do you want?"

The vitamins at the moment were Paw Patrol gummies. The directions said, '*For adults and children 4 years and older, chew two gummies daily.*' So he had the same vitamins she did, letting her pick the two characters of her choice.

"Who do we have today?" Ally asked.

"Looks like Chase, Marshall, Rubble, and Rubble," he replied.

Ally studied them for a moment and then took two. "Chase and Marshall."

"Good picks, my dear," Cary said before he tossed the other two into his mouth and began chewing them. When Ally finished her vitamins and juice, he helped her down to the floor and had her help with breakfast. "Can you get me the mixing bowl?"

Ally went right to the cabinet where the bowls were and selected the pink mixing bowl from the colored set. "Here you go."

Cary pointed to the cabinet where the pancake mix was and said, "How about the pancake mix?"

Ally's eyes lit up and she smiled as she lifted from the ground and floated into the air up to the cabinet.

"Concentrate," Cary said as her body quivered a bit when she went to open the cabinet door.

"I am," Ally replied, steadying herself. She then opened the cabinet door, flying back slightly as she did, then she moved back in so she could reach the pancake mix.

"Fantastic," Cary said, feeling very proud of her and how quickly she was mastering her talents. Some flyers took years to gain as much control as she already had only four months shy of her fifth birthday.

"Thank you," Ally said as she lowered down, trying to

land on the counter with the pancake mix. Before she touched down, the container with the pancake mix hit the counter first, breaking her concentration slightly, and she started to fall. Cary lunged to catch her, but she steadied herself. The container with the pancake mix—which fortunately was in a plastic container instead of the box it had come in—crashed to the floor. "It was an accident."

"I know it was," Cary said. "You caught yourself. You did great."

Ally looked relieved. "Can I try again?"

"With the syrup," Cary said, jabbing his thumb over his shoulder and pointing at a cabinet behind him.

Ally clapped excitedly and then soared back into the air, flying over to the cabinet where the syrup was kept.

Nanny flew into the room, less enthused by the dropped pancake mix container. "What was that crash I heard?"

"Hardly a crash," Cary said as he crouched down to pick up the container. It hadn't even popped open, so none of the pancake mix was wasted.

"Something fell," Nanny said, her robotic gaze firmly set on the container Cary was picking back up. She then shifted her focus to Ally hovering by the cabinet and taking the syrup out. "What if somebody sees her?"

"We're in our house. Facing the woods. She's fine," Cary said dismissively. It was rather funny for Nanny to be so worried and Cary not to be. When it came to Ally, he was extremely protective of her. But he wasn't worried about someone seeing her fly in the privacy of their own home when there were no neighbors who were close enough to glimpse something unexpected.

"Advanced surveillance technology does exist on this world," Nanny pointed out. "Someone could be watching your heat signatures through the walls this very moment."

"Are you growing paranoid, Nanny?" Cary asked as he put the pancake mix next to the bowl. "Nobody is spying on us."

"Now that you two have come out as superheroes, it's only a matter of time," Nanny said.

That was a good point. They were drawing attention to themselves. It was only natural that others would be curious and want to try to get to the bottom of it. But he still felt safe in their own home.

"We could always create a signal jammer, or some kind of shield," Ally suggested.

Cary smiled at her as she flew back to him, landing this time and then putting the syrup on the counter. "Good," he said, acknowledging that she learned from her mistake. "Signal jammer? Shield?"

"I'm sure Nanny and I could tinker something up," Ally said.

"Oh could you?" Cary asked, impressed that she even had the idea.

"Can I, Daddy?"

"Give it a try," Cary said. "Never can be too careful, right? But it can't be anything noticeable to anyone who comes over. That would attract attention, too."

"Okay," Ally agreed.

"Now grab your chair, enough flying for one breakfast, and come over here," Cary said.

They kept a bridge chair in the kitchen that Ally used to stand on when he was teaching her how to cook or bake or she needed to get something high. She brought it over and stood on it. Cary walked her through the instructions on how to make the pancake mix, how to stir it, and then he took over when it was time to actually pour the batter.

While she was still stirring, he grabbed the kettle and asked, "Did you want to stick with juice or would you like hot chocolate?" It was usually an even split with what she would pick, one day it would be more juice, the next it would be hot chocolate.

"Hot chocolate, please," Ally replied.

Cary filled the kettle up a little more. The days it was only him he heated less water than when it was for both of them. He then opened the cabinet to look at the mugs. "Tinkerbell or Baymax today?"

"Baymax," Ally said.

Cary took the mugs down. They had a good twenty mugs to choose from, but he tried to alternate her selections so that they were all being used. He then put the mix in and got the milk ready for hers—he always added milk to hers to make sure it was nice and warm and not too hot.

As soon as the breakfast was cooking, Loveaby peeked her head around the corner. The scent of the food was enough to wake her up and bring her hurrying downstairs.

"Want to feed Loveaby?" Cary asked.

"I do!" Ally replied excitedly. She then went to the refrigerator to get his food and put it in his bowl. For a dragon, he actually enjoyed the dog food that was made on this world, which was quite fortunate. After the food was down and Loveaby was happily chomping away, she emptied his water bowl and filled it with new filtered water.

"Breakfast is ready," Cary said as he put their food on their plates. Dog bone pancakes, scrambled eggs, with a side of freshly cut cantaloupe. He had bacon that he could have made with it, too, but he only added that in upon request, which wasn't all that often. He usually timed it perfectly, so as the pancakes were done, the kettle was whistling too, for their hot chocolates. He finished making their drinks and then brought everything over to the table.

After breakfast was over he filled Ally's bath tub and she got in. He then went back to his bathroom and shaved before taking a shower. They would both brush their teeth together after they were done. She liked to feel independent, but he still liked to make sure she was learning to do

32

things properly. So he would crouch down and they would both brush their teeth together, with Ally seeing what he was doing and mimicking it. He used to always brush his teeth before his shower, but she always wanted her bath first, so he made the adjustment.

A little ding on his phone drew his attention as he was getting dressed. He picked his phone up and saw that there was a new email from Ally's Dance School teacher. "Ally, it's a message from Ms. Lizzie."

"Ms. Lizzie?" Ally said as she rushed in, half dressed herself.

Cary read the email over. "It says here that she has decided not to rebuild Lizzie's Little Dancers, at least not right away. Instead she is going back to the school where she first learned to dance, Awgle Dance and Gymnastics Academy."

"Awful Dance Academy?" Ally asked, her face wrinkled like she smelt something horrible.

"Awgle," Cary corrected. "She said she's there now and hopes that all of her students, you, will decide to go there, too. She's there today. Want to go check it out on the way to the park?"

"I can dance again?"

"Yes you can," Cary said.

"Yay! Let's go. Let's go now, Daddy."

Cary laughed. "Finish getting dressed, and then we'll

33

go."

That was all Ally needed to hear as she ran out of his room to finish getting dressed for the day. When she was done, she was wearing a Minnie Mouse dress that was blue with multi-colored stripes along the bottom, a gray top with Minnie sitting on blue stripes, and pastel-colored hearts in the upper corner. She had white dress shoes on.

"I thought we were going to the park? Don't you want sneakers?" Cary asked.

"I'm fine like this," Ally replied.

He used to lay out all of her clothes, matching colors and patterns and putting everything together for her. She liked to do it herself now, and she always did an amazing job of matching things, just like he had done. But white shoes for a playground? "How about you grab a sweatshirt in case you get cold, and some socks and shoes just in case?"

"Okay, Daddy," Ally said as she returned to her room to get some extra things for their day.

They packed the car with a bag of extra clothes just in case, extra jackets, hat, gloves, and scarf—it was still February in Massachusetts, after all! He also had a bag of snacks, a Little Mermaid umbrella, her blankey, a book to read, her Kindle to play on, and several of her friends—toys—that she wanted to bring with her. And then they were off on their latest adventure!

34

CHAPTER

The drive to Lizzie's Little Dancers were a mere five minutes. Cary plugged the address in for Awgle Dance and Gymnastics Academy and was pleasantly surprised to see that it was only 3.8 miles from their new house, and according to his GPS nine minutes. That wasn't bad at all.

"And away we go," Cary said as they backed out of the garage and onto the driveway. "On the road again."

Ally chimed in, joining him, "Do de do dah do de dah. Just can't wait to get on the road again."

"I love you," Cary said. "Have I told you that lately?"

"Yes," Ally replied.

"Good, I don't want you to ever forget!"

The GPS sent them down a few back roads they had never been down before, then through a residential neighborhood with some really nice houses. At the end of the road was a sign for the new Dance School. Cary pulled into the parking lot. The old school was in a little outdoor mall with a stage and everything. This one was a big building by itself.

"This looks like it," Cary said. "You excited?"

"Yeah!" Ally shouted.

Cary reached back and unbuckled her car seat. She then crawled into the front and had him pick her up and take her out of the car. They walked inside and saw dozens of kids, most in dance outfits, all about. There was a woman at a table that was set up, a room behind her with the door open and kids inside looking at outfits.

The woman looked up at him. "May I help you?"

Cary set Ally down. "Yes, we're from Lizzie's Little Dancers and got an email to come here to register."

"Oh yes, we're doing an open house this weekend to register new dancers," the woman explained. "All new dancers will get added into the classes that we were teaching."

"Will she be behind?" Cary asked.

"She'll be fine," the woman said. "Here's a list of options. Want to take a look at it and then come back over to fill out the registration?"

"Sure," Cary said, taking the pamphlet from her.

He and Ally went and sat down at chairs that were set up around the edges of the waiting area. He scanned it and found Tap and Ballet, two of the things she was taking at Lizzie's on Wednesdays, the same night she had it before. It was under the Shining Stars section, which was four and five year olds. There were four options: Tap, Ballet, Jazz and Hip Hop, and Gymnastics. They could register for a combo, with a two-way combo for one hour a week, a three-way combo for an hour and a half a week, or a four-way combo for two hours a week. To have what she had would be the two-way combo, he assumed.

"What do you think? Did you want the same things you were doing?" Cary asked.

"Yeah," Ally replied.

"Do you want to try this one, too?" he asked, then read the description for Jazz and Hip Hop, "High energy-fast moving feel good class that teaches the hottest dance moves of today through technique of jazz. You learn combinations as seen on some of the most popular music videos. Age appropriate music and choreography are used, ensuring to excite and exercise the mind and body."

"I want to do that," Ally said.

"Okay, so all three then? Add that to Tap and Ballet?"

"Yeah," Ally said.

"You got it," Cary said. He walked back over to the woman, Ally right by his side, and they reviewed the schedule on Wednesdays for the three. He then signed Ally up for Tap at 4:00, Ballet at 4:30, and Jazz and Hip Hop at 5:00.

"Here's a list of the shoes and tights you will need," the woman said, handing him a piece of paper. There were specific models and colors for shoes and tights listed. "Go into the room behind me and we'll have her fitted for her leotard."

"She can't use the ones she already has?" Cary asked.

"Everyone wears the same one per class here at the Academy," she said.

"A uniform," Cary replied. "Okay." That was too bad. Ally loved alternating her outfits and picking out what she wanted to wear week to week to Dance School. Now all of those outfits would just be for at home.

They went into the next room where another woman greeted them. She took Ally's measurements and then selected an aqua-blue leotard for her. "Try this one."

Cary took it and was shown where the bathrooms were. He and Ally went into the bathroom and she tried the leotard on. It fit fine. They came back out and he saw another parent looking at shorts, too. "What are the shorts?" he asked.

"Oh, those are optional," the woman said. "She can wear them if she'd like."

He picked one up. They were black and had rhinestones forming the letters ADG, for Awgle Dance and Gymnastics, just dropping off the last A for Academy. "What do you think? Do you want the shorts, too?"

"Yeah," Ally said.

"Okay, we'll take the shorts, too," Cary said.

As he was paying, Ally's attention was drawn to something at the end of the hall. She took a few steps, paused, and then said, "I want to do that!"

Cary finished paying, took a bag with their things, and then walked over to join her. At the end of the hall was a giant gym with balance beams and adjustable bars and uneven bars and spring boards and wall crawling and tumble tracks and mats everywhere. Kids were running along the floor and then doing multiple backflips in succession before landing with their arms raised.

"Ms. Lizzie!" Ally shouted.

Cary followed her gaze and saw her working with some of the girls in the gym. She heard Ally and waved them over. So they went to go say hello.

"That was impressive," Cary said.

"The floor, it's springy," Lizzie explained, bouncing up and down, almost like on a trampoline.

"Can I do that?" Ally asked.

Cary looked at Lizzie questioningly. "Is she too young for that?"

"No. She's at a good age to get started."

"We already registered though," Cary said.

"Aw," Ally said, disappointed.

"They'll let you switch. What did you take?" Lizzie asked.

"We got the three-way combo of Tap, Ballet, and Jazz and Hip Hop," Cary said. "Is there one of those she should skip? She thought Jazz sounded like fun, so I don't want to take that away."

Lizzie nodded, understandingly. "She'll need ballet, but she's already got the fundamentals. She can finish out the year with it. Do gymnastics instead of ballet. That's what Tanya is doing."

Cary was glad to hear that. Tanya was also from Lizzie's Little Dancers, and one of Ally's friends. She was also Lizzie's daughter, so if Tanya was skipping ballet for the rest of the year, then it was probably okay for Ally to do the same.

"What do you think? Do you want to skip ballet? Just like Tanya?" Cary asked.

"Can I be in the same classes as Tanya?" Ally asked.

"When did you sign up?" Lizzie asked.

"Wednesdays. 4:00 to 5:30," Cary said.

"Let's go look," Lizzie said. She told the girls she'd be right back and then led them back to the registration desk. She glanced and said, "I think if she takes gymnastics at 4:30 she'll be in the same classes as Tanya."

"Can we make a change?" Cary asked.

"Of course," the woman at registration said. She then went over it, with Lizzie selecting the classes and making the adjustment. The woman took the shoes and supplies list back and crossed off the ballet slippers. "All set to start this week."

"Thanks," Cary said. He stepped away from the desk and asked Lizzie, "Are the rest of the kids coming here? Erin? The twins?"

"I haven't seen anyone else yet," Lizzie said. "But it's early."

"Well, hopefully everyone will come over. Thanks for letting us know."

"Of course." She then crouched down. "I'll see you on Wednesday, Ally."

"See you on Wednesday," she said back.

Cary and Ally headed back to the car, got settled back in, and put the address for the Dance School supply store in Milford into their GPS. "Might as well go get your shoes on the way to the park."

A short drive to the store and the salesperson there was very helpful, sizing Ally's feet and then bringing out the Tap and Jazz shoes that were identified on the list from their new Dance Academy. They picked up some more tights, colorful ones rather than the traditional tan so Ally could still have some individuality, and then were back on the road in no time at all.

"Who is ready for the playground?" Cary asked.

"Me!" Ally shouted.

CHAPTER

5

The park that Cary was heading for was actually attached to the elementary school in Heidi's hometown of Holliston. He was sure that the parks in Bellingham were fine, but Heidi mentioned how this one was different and could only be used when school was out of session. Since it was February vacation, an unusually warm February vacation at that, this was the perfect opportunity to check it out. Besides, he and Ally liked exploring, so finding a new playground was perfect.

When they pulled in, there wasn't a single other car in the parking lot. No kids on the playground at all. They had the place completely to themselves. Cary glanced around, wondering if there was any way people could see them if he let Ally practice her new powers out in the open. They were far enough back from the road, behind the school, so nobody would see them unless she flew higher than the building. On the other side of the park was a hill and woods, so he didn't see houses or stores where someone might look out the window. She might just be able to fly as long as nobody else came.

The playground itself was all red and black. The supports and any ropes or chains were all black, everything else—from stairs to slides to platforms hanging from ropes to try to cross to monkey bars to a giant spider web to climb to swings and plenty more—was red.

"What do you think?" Cary asked.

"Good!" Ally replied enthusiastically.

Cary leaned back and unfastened her car seat buckles. Ally then climbed into the front seat onto his lap for them to get out together. "Want to switch to sneakers first?"

"I'm fine," Ally said.

White shoes it was. He then opened the door and got out, holding her in his arms. They walked over to the park and he set her down. "You can try using your powers unless someone else comes, okay?"

Her eyes lit up. "I can?"

"But if I say to stop, do so immediately. Deal?"

"Deal," she said.

"Have fun," he said as she ran off. He followed along, staying close to her and taking the occasional picture as she attempted each of the things at the park. She was only young once and he loved capturing those gorgeous smiles so that they would always be able to look back and remember how happy she was growing up. He hoped, especially with her now being a superhero, that whatever challenges life presented that she would always keep that smile on her face and have love and joy in her heart.

One of the slides had all rollers, so as she slid down she rolled down. She giggled and flew back to the top to do it again, glancing at her Daddy to make sure it was still all right to do so. Cary smiled at her and nodded. She then slid down again, laughing as she bumped from roller to roller down the slide.

"This is so much fun!" she shouted. She slid down one more time and then ran to him, holding her hand out for his. "Can you come with me?"

"Of course," he said. Especially when it was just the two of them. When there were more kids around he usually would tell her to have fun and just watch. He didn't mind going down slides with her or swinging on swings, but he didn't know if other kids or other parents would mind, so when others showed up he just stayed close in case she needed him and took pictures for the memories. But being alone, it was time to be a kid again himself!

He got up on the slide and slid down, feeling the bumps and shouting, "Wheeeee!!!!" as he went down, only with each roller his voice changed octaves, causing Ally to laugh again.

"You're funny, Daddy."

"Thank you, honey."

Done with the slides, she ran over to the swings and got on. Usually she would ask him to come push her, and that she wanted to go higher and faster, but this time she started up on her own and nearly squealed in delight as she shouted, "I'm doing it! Daddy, I'm doing it!"

"Amazing!" he said, feeling so proud of her. "Great job!"

"I'm a big girl now!" she shouted as she swung higher.

He had to chuckle at that. She felt old enough to wear a costume, fly around, and try to help people, but the simple things in life were still fundamental and consistent across the board. Here she was, a little girl who was a little over four and a half, excited that she could finally swing on the swing without help. That feeling of accomplishment, of independence, for a little girl, it was like winning the lottery. She was doing something she previously couldn't, and she was loving every moment of it.

Cary heard a car pulling up. Even though Ally hadn't been flying much while playing, he quickly said to her, "All done with flying."

"Okay, Daddy," she said, still swinging on the swings.

The vehicle was a red SUV, larger than the Trax that he and Ally drove up in. Two women and three kids—two girls and a boy—got out. The little boy came running right for the playground, whereas the girls stayed near the truck.

"Daddy, help me stop," Ally said.

Cary reached out for the chain and slowed the swing down. Once it came to a stop, Ally jumped off and ran right for the little boy. Cary walked after her.

She ran right up to him and said, "Hi, I'm Ally. What's your name?"

The little boy had a tanned complexion, brown hair and matching brown eyes. He smiled at Ally, said, "I'm Sign," and then ran for the ladder to climb up and begin playing.

Ally followed after him, slid down the slide with him, and then said, "Come this way. Try this one," leading him over to the slide with the rollers.

"Okay," Sign said, following her to the other slide. Both bounced down the rollers as they slid down and giggled together.

The others walked over. The two women, presumably

the mothers, sat on a bench and talked to each other. The two girls were riding scooters.

Cary could tell that Ally was enamored with the scooters as she stared at them and watched the two girls riding along the pavement between the school and the playground. She then made her way over to them, and said again, "Hi, I'm Ally, what's your name?"

Unlike Sign, these girls did not seem to want to make a new friend.

"Come on, let's go over there," one of them said to the other, and they rode away on their scooters.

Ally was not deterred though, as she ran after them. "Can I try?"

One girl, with a similar complexion to Sign, stopped her scooter, looked at Ally, and scoffed. "You're too little to ride a scooter. Go away."

Ally's head immediately dropped, her chin to her chest, as she turned around and headed back to her Daddy. Cary could see how hurt she was. Knew she was fighting back tears. When she got to him, the pain threatened to break through as she said, "All I wanted to do was be nice. Why won't they share?"

He had always told her that whatever was his was also hers. That was fine for a family, but when playing with others, sometimes people did not want to share. When it was something that was theirs, that was entirely their decision.

"Honey, she doesn't know you. Maybe she's afraid you'd get hurt, or break it."

"But I won't," she pouted.

"I know that. You know that. But it's her scooter. That makes it her decision," Cary said, while hugging her, hoping that she would understand.

His eyes drifted up, looking at the two girls as they rode by, mocking her and shouting things like, "I know you couldn't do this!" or "No way you can handle this!" Kids could be cruel sometimes. They don't want her to ride the scooter, fine. But to then taunt her and rub it in? That wasn't nice.

Cary let Ally out of his hug and focused on the hill and woods behind the park. "Want to go exploring with me?"

Her eyes lit up again, the scooters already forgotten about. "Yeah!"

They went through the park and up the hill. On the other side was a steep decline with leaves completely covering it. But it they followed the hill further down, it looked like it wasn't as steep and there was even a path. "Let's go this way."

Ally followed.

The path had a big sign by it, saying that this was conservation land. The path seemed to go through the woods and extended for quite some time. Ally climbed up on a big rock, turned, and smiled. "Look at me!"

"Look at you!" Cary said, then "Smile!" as he snapped a few more pictures. Not that he needed to prompt her to smile, but that way at least she knew he was taking a picture and wouldn't climb down before he got it.

They followed the path for a little bit, exploring, talking, laughing, but then Ally got bored and said, "Can we go home?"

"Sure," Cary said. He then glanced at the steep incline with the leaves. He didn't want her going down it afraid that she might fall, but going up, it looked like a fun little challenge. "How about we climb the hill?"

"Can we?" Ally asked.

"Absolutely," Cary said, snapping a few pictures of her as she made her way up—appearing to be completely immersed in a world of leaves—and then began climbing up himself. They both got to the top without any real issues, though the steeper it got, the more he planted his foot so she could lean against him and keep climbing without slipping backwards. But they made it just fine.

"That was fun," she said.

"I thought so, too," Cary said. "Come on, let's get going."

On the way back to the car though, the same girl that

was mean to her rode over on her scooter and came to a stop. "Here, do you want to try it?"

Cary instantly felt the hairs on the back of his neck rise. Why did this little girl suddenly change her mind? Was she going to do something like pull it back at the last second, or try to trip Ally and hurt her? He was instantly in protector mode and didn't want his little girl's feelings to get hurt again. But Ally clapped her hands and ran over, and to his surprise, the little girl handed over the scooter and then stepped away.

Ally rode the scooter for a couple of minutes, riding it like she had always been on one even though she had never touched one before. Cary snapped a few more pictures of her riding, making sure he got a nice zoomed in close up when she was facing him to capture her smile. Then she rode back to the little girl, got off, and very politely thanked her. The girl took it back and rode away.

When they got back to their car, Ally said, "She was a nice little girl after all."

"I'm glad," Cary said. "Did you have a good time?"

"Yeah!" Ally shouted.

"Are you hungry?" he asked.

"I'm hungry," Ally confirmed.

"Do you want me to cook at home, or should we stop somewhere?"

Ally considered it for a moment, and then said, "Cook at home."

"You got it," Cary said. He then buckled her back into her car seat, put her blanket on her legs—even though it was warm out she still liked the feeling of it on her legs—and handed her one of her stuffed animals and her Kindle. He then went around the car, got in, started it up, and headed back home. A busy morning. He suspected that Ally would be ready for a pretty lengthy nap after lunch today. He could use one, too. That sounded delightful.

CHAPTER 6

The weather was too good to be true. Heidi's words about typical New England weather and changing patterns came to be prophetic. In a matter of days, they went from seventies to a blizzard with winds so severe that trees were being torn from the ground and toppling everywhere. One could hardly move anywhere without seeing an endless flow of white snow with whiteout conditions or fallen trees and branches. Even things like trampolines were lifted right up and sent scurrying—he found Ally's in the woods behind their house.

While the snow and wind would be bad enough, the

fallen trees and branches were covered so quickly that they were often difficult to see. Even the crews that were out plowing and shoveling could not work quickly enough to notice everything that had come down, and more than a few plows wound up getting stuck and needing help as they rammed into a tree or branch and could not force their way back out of it.

Naturally, for a pair of superheroes, that presented an opportunity to go help out. If only it wasn't so cold! A bristling cold that chilled you deep to the core no matter how many layers you wore. With the incessant snowfall, it was hard to see even your own hand in front of your face. This was quite the introduction to winters in New England, to be sure.

Ally sat by the window next to the fireplace and stared out, straining to see. Cary was never one to watch the news, but it was on and they could see reporters standing in the snow and cautioning people to stay indoors. A State of Emergency was issued and motorists were instructed to stay off of the roads to allow plows and emergency services to do their jobs.

"Want to go shovel for a bit with me?" Cary asked. He had bought Ally a child-sized shovel with Disney Princesses on it.

"Yeah!" Ally shouted.

The two bundled up in layers, with Nanny swirling overhead and objecting to their going out, and then headed to
the garage. Cary pushed the button to open the garage
door, and in seconds a cold gust of air blew inside with
snow flowing into the opening. A lot of houses, Heidi said,
had people who plowed them out, but this was their first
major snowstorm on this planet and they had not hired
anyone yet. So it was all shoveling for them. But while the
snow was overpowering, Cary could see how fascinated Ally
was by it. This could be fun.

"Let's see if we can make a dent," Cary said.

The snow was already up to Ally's waist and was showing no sign of slowing. If nothing else, it would be good to
help try to get ahead of the storm by shoveling now so the
next time it wouldn't be so bad. Cary suspected that they,
or at least he since this was way too deep for Ally to really
be able to contribute, would have to come out a few times
before the storm was done.

Cary would shovel, going from the garage door straight
to the grass on the other side of the driveway, then walk
back. Ally would shovel the new snow that was landing on
the spots where Cary had already done, or when the snow
slid off the shovel and was still on the driveway. After working at it for about an hour, the section in front of the garage
doors were cleared, but the rest of the driveway was still

only partially done.

It was too cold to stay out this long. Ally had gone in a few times to warm up, but Cary thought it was a good time for some hot chocolate and to warm up by the fireplace. They certainly had made their dent. That was good enough for now. He could see Ally trembling from the cold. She was shivering. The rest could wait.

"Let's head back inside. Warm up," Cary said.

"Okay," Ally replied, her teeth chattering.

The two got inside the garage and Cary pushed the button to close the door. They then walked inside the house and removed their wet layers. He then dried Ally off with a towel. "Go sit by the fire. I'll make us some hot chocolate and then start a hot bath for you."

"Yay!" Ally said.

"Do you want the princess tub or the hot tub?" he asked, seeing which bathtub she wanted. Her bathroom had full Disney Princess décor with the shower liner, hand towels, bath towel, toothbrush, rinsing cup, and floor mat. The bathmat wasn't princess, but was Minnie Mouse sitting on a beach, so similar themed. In his bathroom he had a whirlpool tub with the jets to circulate the water. The décor was more beach themed with sea shells and star fish and light ocean-blue colors. But the tub was bigger, had the jets, and she could swim in it and play more.

"Hot tub," she said.

"Hot tub it is," Cary replied. He put the kettle on and then headed upstairs and started the water. He got a towel for her, this time Elsa and Anna from Frozen, which seemed appropriate for the snow, and set it on the counter. He then headed back down and joined her by the fire, giving her a big hug for warmth. "Feeling warmer?"

"Much," she said. "I have an idea."

"Oh?" Cary asked.

"We should have Loveaby clear the driveway," Ally said.

Cary shifted his gaze to the little dragon sound asleep on the couch. "Loveaby?"

"Yeah, he could just breathe fire and melt it," Ally suggested.

Cary grinned at that. An interesting idea. "I love you so much."

"I love you more," Ally said.

The kettle began to whistle. Cary got up to get it off of the stove and finished making their hot chocolates. He brought a mug back to Ally. "Here you go."

After they got a few sips in, he headed upstairs to check on the tub to make sure it wasn't close to overflowing. The water was over the spouts for the jets, so he turned it off and checked the water. Nice and warm.

He headed back down and joined her. "The bath is ready for whenever you're done with your hot chocolate. No rush. Enjoy it."

"Okay," Ally said.

A few more sips and they both jerked their heads toward the window after hearing a loud noise.

"What was that?" Ally asked.

Cary strained to see through the snow outside the window but could not make anything out. "I can't see anything. Nanny, can your sensors detect anything?"

Nanny hovered by the window, humming softly. "There has been an accident." Nanny replied after a pause. She emitted a holographic image of a truck that had skidded off of the road and was stuck in the snow, a fallen tree limb pinning the plow down.

"We can help," Ally said.

"Are you warm enough?" Cary asked.

"I am good," Ally replied.

The two donned their costumes and went out through the garage doors again. The snow was so bad that Cary doubted that anyone would be able to see them even if they were standing at the bottom of the driveway.

"Hold onto me," Cary said. He waited for Ally to get a good grip around his neck, and then he jumped up into the air. The snow pelted their faces and stung as they soared through the air, but they landed quickly right by the accident. "Let him know we're here to help."

"I'm on it," Little Bluey said as she flew over to the window and knocked. The man was inside, shaken up, but conscious.

"Is he okay?"

"He looks okay," Little Bluey said. She knocked again and the man rolled the window down, looking at her curiously. "Hi, I'm Little Bluey. Are you okay?"

"Hit something," the man said, still appearing dumbfounded to be seeing a little girl hovering by his window. "I think I'm seeing things."

Little Bluey held up three fingers. "How many fingers am I holding up?"

"What?"

"How many fingers?" Little Bluey asked again, pointing at her hand with the three fingers up.

"Three," he said, clearly still in shock.

Little Bluey glanced and saw that her Daddy had freed the plow from the branch and was then moving behind the truck. "Hold onto something."

"What?" he asked, but then he gasped and grabbed for his wheel as the entire truck lifted up into the air and then was set down on the street. "How?"

"That's my Daddy," Little Bluey said, all smiles.

The man looked in his side mirror and saw Boston Bluey step out from behind the truck.

"Do you have a cell phone?" Boston Bluey asked.

"What?"

"A cell phone," Little Bluey said, still smiling warmly.

"Yes," the man said.

"You're on the road, but you should probably still get your truck towed and have someone look you over to make sure you're okay," Boston Bluey said.

"O... okay," the man said. "Thank you."

"Anytime," Boston Bluey said, walking back to the front of the truck and lifting another limb that had fallen and tossed it to the side of the road.

Little Bluey nodded encouragingly, and then added, "Good to go. Bye." She then flew over to her father, wrapped her arms around his neck, and he jumped up into the storm and they were gone just like that.

"Ready for your bath?" He asked.

"Can we try to help someone else?"

Cary nodded. "Of course we can. But only for a little bit. I don't want you to catch a cold."

Boston Bluey and Little Bluey did stay out to help, freeing a few plows and helping some cars that skidded off of the roads, but the storm was so bad that they ultimately came home for another hot chocolate and to sit before their own fire and wait out the storm. It was so cold and the wind was brutal and the snow never ending. This certainly was no place for a four-year-old girl, even if she could fly. The town's emergency services had handled weather like this long before they ever heard of Boston Bluey and Little Bluey, and Cary wanted to make sure that his little girl didn't get hurt or sick trying to do too much in these conditions.

Unfortunately, there was someone else out in these conditions, someone hoping that Little Bluey would come to his rescue. Someone she did not know needed help...

✶   ✶   ✶

"Thank you, Greg. This is Evie Berman, WTB TV and the on sight reporter during what is easily the storm of the decade. With high winds and snow increasing in intensity, it is really bad out there, and storm conditions are getting significantly worse. The forecast shows that things are going to continue to deteriorate. The Governor has issued a State of Emergency and asks everyone to please stay indoors. If you can see through the swirling winds and snow behind me, the roads are barren as people adhere to the storm warnings. Only plows and emergency vehicles are braving these elements.

"Earlier this evening, several motorists reported that they had been rescued by our local superheroes, Boston and Little Bluey."

The image shifted to earlier that evening with Evie Berman interviewing a man with a beard and a yellow emergency vest on. "Evie Berman, WTB TV, I am here with Jack Simms, a town plow operator, who found his truck run off road and stuck after hitting a fallen limb of a tree. He thought his evening would be wasted as he waited for help, but it came sooner than he anticipated. Mister Simms, could you tell us what happened?"

"Yeah, um, I was driving my plow and then I struck something. You know, there are downed trees and branches everywhere with this wind and wet snow. I didn't even see it, and after I hit, I swerved off the road into a snow-covered ditch."

"What happened then?"

"Well, the strangest thing. This little girl in a pink mask was floating beside my truck and knocked on my window. She said that I should brace myself. Then my truck began to move. Sideways, mind you."

"Did you see what it was?"

"Yeah, a guy dressed up like he was one of those comic movie characters. I wouldn't believe it if I didn't see it, but he was moving my rig all by himself, as easily as if he were just pushing a snowblower. It seemed effortless. But he got me back on the road, then lifted the branch out of the road and tossed it aside like it was nothing. The little girl knocked again and said I was good to go. Just like that. Good to go. Uncanny."

"And there you have it, our resident superheroes are braving the elements to help out where they can. This is Evie Berman, WTB TV, back to you, Greg."

The image shifted back to Evie in the storm. "And there you have it. Several motorists and police reports have indicated sightings of Boston and Little Bluey. If we have any new news, we'll be the first on scene to report it. In the meantime, stay home, stay safe, stay warm. This is Evie Berman, WTB TV, back to you, Greg."

Sign shut the television off and ran over to the door, fumbling with his snowsuit to get it on and then zipped it up. He then slipped on his boots, his hat, a scarf around his mouth, and finished with his gloves.

"Where do you think you're going?"

Sign turned to see Signah standing behind him, rotating the crystal dangling from her necklace between her index finger and thumb. "Didn't you hear, Little Bluey is out to-night!"

"So what?" Signah asked.

"So I want to try and see her."

63

"The odds of you seeing her are slim to none," Signah said bluntly. "What makes you think she'll come anywhere near here?"

"I have to try," Sign said.

"You're not supposed to go out in this weather," Signah added.

"That's driving." Sign replied, pleased with himself for knowing that people were supposed to stay off of the roads.

"I'll tell Mom."

Sign paused at that, then his gaze shifted to find his mother asleep on the couch. "Don't you dare!"

"I will."

"You won't wake her," Sign said, trying to act more confident than he felt.

Signah did hesitate, then said, "Fine, go get yourself all frostbitten. You don't need toes or fingers or a nose anyway." She stuck her tongue out at him, pivoted, and stormed off.

Sign considered it a personal victory that she had backed down. His sister rarely backed down from anything. He opened the door and stepped outside, greeted by howling winds and snow pelting him in the face. He wished he had the goggles that skiers wore. He tried to shield his eyes with his arms, but he couldn't see anything.

He began to turn back to go inside. Signah was right. It

was too bad out. He wouldn't see Little Bluey even if she were flying three feet in front of him. But then he stopped. He had finally won an argument with his sister. If he walked right back inside, he knew exactly what she would say. "I told you so." Or at least some variant of that. His victory would turn into a defeat real quick. He couldn't go back in. At least not so quickly.

Sign trudged through the ever mounting snow. They had all shoveled not too long ago, and already the walkway was fully covered as if they had never even been outside. He wished he had brought his shovel with him. But he kept pushing on.

"Little Bluey!" he shouted, though even he had to admit that nobody would hear him. "Little Bluey, are you out there?"

Sign headed down to the street. In front of their house was a stone wall that had been here since the house was built nearly half a century before. The wall was covered in snow, but he knew where it was because the snow flowed up and was higher there. He stepped up onto it and strained to see. It was hopeless.

Above him he heard a creak as the wind pounded at him and everything around him. It was time to go back inside. The creak turned to a crack, and Sign looked up as the old Willow Tree in the front yard toppled over and landed right on top of him.

Sign was trapped. It was so cold. He could not move, pinned down. He could feel the icy branches above and somehow he was pushed down enough where he could feel the stone beneath the snow. His legs hurt. His arms hurt. His whole body hurt. Then the cold numbness began to take over.

"Help," he said, but the word did not come easily to him. It was more like a muffled cry. He tried again. "Help." Still soft. He then closed his eyes and prayed, "Little Bluey, please find me. Help me, please help me." But no matter how much he wished to will it, no matter how many times he thought she would be there any moment to save him, no matter how many times he imagined that she was really there, she never did come. He was alone. Trapped. Helpless. And there was nobody to come save him.

"Sign!"

He struggled to open his eyes. They were frozen and covered with wet snow that was quickly turning to ice. Did he really hear something? Was it her? Was it Little Bluey?

"Sign! Where are you?"

Not Little Bluey... it was Signah.

"Sign! Answer me!"

Sign tried to reply. "Over here." The words were clear in his mind, but only a choked gurgle escaped his lips.

"Sign!"

She was getting closer. Why didn't Little Bluey come and save him? Why had she abandoned him?

"Sign!"

She was real close now. But it didn't matter. Signah was not a superhero. She wouldn't be able to help him.

"Sign! I'm here. Sign, it's me!"

Her hand touched his, but he could not feel it. He tried to speak again, but the words escaped him. All he could do was look at her and shiver.

"Sign, I won't leave you. I'm here. I'll save you."

If only she had left him. If only she had gone for help. Maybe at least she would have been okay. It had already been too late for him. But neither of their lives would ever be the same again. The night of the blizzard, the storm of the decade, the moment dreams died and superheroes failed to protect those in need. It was the night a boy filled with compassion and hope and dreams instead found himself fueled by anger and resentment and spite.

CHAPTER 7

The best part of snow storms in New England could be well debated. Was it the nice hot mug of hot chocolate on a cold day? Was it sitting by the roaring fireplace and relaxing? Was it going outside and having an adventure playing in the snow? With as much snow as they had, people were advised to continue to stay home. Power was out across much of the state and crews were working around the clock trying to restore it. For Ally and her Daddy, none of that mattered. They enjoyed their hot chocolates by the fire, and then they were ready to brave the outdoors.

Heidi helped them out by setting them up with Walt

Mulvey. He was the son of one of her childhood friends and had started up his own landscaping company, Picture Perfect Properties. Cary liked the idea of giving some work to someone just starting out, so he stopped by several times during the day to plow the driveway as someone who was making the rounds with him got out to shovel the walkway to the front door.

Ally, naturally, wanted to see everything that was happening, so they opened the garage door so she could watch. Cary had a couple of bottles of water ready to go and offered them to Walt and the person shoveling.

"How is it out there?" Cary asked.

"Brutal," Walt said. "Roads are horrible. Visibility is awful."

"Can I get you anything else? A snack? Something?" Cary asked.

"No, we're good, thanks for the waters," Walt replied.

"Stay safe out there," Cary said, stepping back into the garage and letting Walt get back to the driveway. They worked quickly. By the time he was done with the driveway, the boy with him, who looked like he must have been in High School, was done with the walkway. Cary waved goodbye to them and then closed the garage door.

"That truck is big," Ally said.

"Big enough to plow," Cary said. It was a new truck,

though the last time Walt had been by and Cary went out he had been told that they were actually about to buy a second truck and he was adding staff to increase the number of people he could service. Storms like this surely were good for business.

When Walt was there, the snow was still coming down. Not as heavy as it had been thus far, but more of a light dusting. With the howling wind though, it still blew it around quite a bit and made things tricky. About an hour later though, things began to clear up and the sun made it's way through the clouds and snow.

"Looks like we're through the worst of it," Cary said.

"Can we go play outside?" Ally asked.

"Absolutely," Cary said.

They had a new snow tube that he blew up for them. He then made sure Ally had several layers of clothes on before they went out and braved the snow. Unlike their superhero costumes that were temperature controlled, they needed to bulk up and be warm. Ally got her layers on, finished up with a full body snowsuit, hat, gloves, and boots, and then she was ready to go. Cary then did his layers, grabbed a shovel, and opened the sliding door to the back porch.

"We'll head out this way."

Unlike the driveway that was plowed or the front walkway that was shoveled, the porch was still full of snow. It trailed half way up the sliding door, so when he slid it open some fell into the house. He could clean it later. That was fine.

"Daddy, it's so high," Ally said.

"I can shovel a path if you'd like," Cary replied.

Ally stared at the snow and nodded. "But only a little."

He could see her holding onto the snow tube and understood. She wanted to slide, but she had to have a way to get to what should have been the stairs.

"You got it."

Cary then began shoveling to get out of the door. When there was a little room to walk, he turned back. "Care to help me?"

"Yeah I do!" Ally said. She then ran to grab her Disney Princesses shovel. She came back out and excitedly began shoveling. The snow was almost as tall as she was, but she didn't mind as she kept working at it. Cary tried to shovel a little off the top and then let Ally shovel the bottom. Ultimately they tried to move it off the porch—which was probably a good idea anyway to reduce the weight—and that itself created a nice little hill for Ally to slide down.

Cary got Ally on the snow tube, made sure she was holding onto the grips, and said, "Are you ready?"

"I'm ready!"

"On three," Cary said. "One, two, three!"

On three he gave the tube a little shove and Ally slid down into the yard, shouting, "Wheee!!!!" the entire time. "Again! Again!"

Cary went down into the snow, trudging through it, to get to Ally. He then slid her along the snow. It was harder than it looked, even with his strength. The snow tube, which had been full of air, seemed to shrink down when it was outside and wasn't flowing as smoothly as it was the longer they were outside.

"Again! Again!" Ally shouted again.

Cary was only too happy to oblige, sometimes pushing the tube, sometimes trying to run through the snow and drag it along with him. The entire time she was giggling and laughing and having the time of her life.

After they were done with the snow tube they made their way over to her swingset and even with snow all over it, Ally got on the swing and began swinging a bit. When she was tired of that she wanted to go down the slide into the snow. After a few times sliding, she was starting to get cold.

"Daddy, I want to go back inside."

"You got it," Cary said. They made their way back through the snow. Cary made sure he had the snow tube and shovels and then closed up the door. "Let's get you out of those wet clothes."

He helped Ally remove her layers and then had her go sit in front of the fireplace. Fortunately, while a lot of houses and neighborhoods were without power, they still had theirs. He went up and prepared a nice hot bath for her in the hot tub. When it was ready she excitedly jumped in and played with her toys while the warm water warmed her back up.

"Are you hungry?" Cary asked.

Ally put her fingers together with a little gap between them. "I'm hungry this much."

"That much? Got it. I'll go make us something for lunch." On a cold day like this, he made some nice Chicken Noodle Soup for them, and had it ready for when she was done with her bath.

"Daddy, this is de-lish."

"De-lish?"

"De-lish," Ally repeated.

"I love you," Cary said, smiling at her. "Have I told you that recently?"

"Yes."

"Good," Cary added. "I wouldn't want you to ever forget."

CHAPTER

8

Techniarch entered the hospital looking just like anybody else. He had evolved to be the master of all technological things. He could understand and communicate with machines in a way that no other could ever hope to grasp. Using that knowledge has always served him well, and in instances like this, he was able to have nanites flowing through his bloodstream modify his outward appearance so that even Protector Archer would never recognize him if he stood in front of him. He could become anyone. Become anything. It was as easy for him as blinking one's eyes.

The news was full of tragedy. Juicy little tidbits of knowledge that he could seek to exploit. Protector Archer and his daughter had been the victim of his portal to bring them to this world, but he still had to manufacture their undoing. Archer was alone here. Vulnerable. Techniarch would take advantage of that and make sure the former Protector was never able to return back home. The next step in his plan was about to commence.

Back in the reality where he had come from, he had used his abilities to warp the minds of others to do his bidding. It was more than manipulation, it was akin to programming. But he also could use technology to rewrite one's very own DNA, tweaking their powers and abilities to suit his needs.

Archer, as a Protector, had hurt him once. He then dedicated his life to hurting him in return. Techniarch took pleasure from Archer's pain and suffering. He did not need recognition or for Archer to ever know that he was behind these plans, or just what he had done to him, but he would always be there plotting his demise.

His image shifted as he rounded a corner and he was fully dressed as a nurse just like the ones who were working. He got some pleasant nods or smiles, but nobody bothered him or asked what he was doing or why he was there. He was blending in. He was very good at blending in.

He found a terminal and sat down. Computers were antiquated in this reality, but a simple touch and he bypassed all security safeguards and found what he was looking for. The children were here. He stood up and began heading to their room, the visage of a nurse shifting into one of a female doctor.

N N N

The hospital had been quite accommodating, allowing Sign and Signah to share a room. Everyone was quite sympathetic for the poor children who were trapped under a tree in the storm and fell victim to frostbite. Their skin colors, even with weeks of efforts to help them, still resembled a murky bluish gray. Sign had lost his limbs. Signah had no feeling in her entire body but they were trying to save her as best they could.

The doctor, one Signah had never seen before, walked in. It was a lady doctor, standing tall and confident. The doctor did not say anything, but looked at each of them one at a time. It was hard for Signah to follow the doctor with her eyes as it hurt her eyelids to move. She would have asked Sign what the doctor was doing, but he was sleeping, even if from his whimpers she knew he was trapped in yet another nightmare.

Sign jerked up with a scream.

"Good, you're awake," the doctor said.

"Who are you?" Sign asked.

"A doctor," Signah said sarcastically. She could no longer roll her eyes, but she refused to lose who she was deep down.

"Yes, a doctor," the doctor said. She then looked intently at Sign. "I hear that Little Bluey failed to save you."

Signah was outraged. Was this doctor taunting them. "Leave him alone."

"I heard it on the news," the doctor said. "And everyone is talking about it. How Little Bluey just had to know where you were but didn't think it was important enough to come help you out."

Who was this doctor? Signah wondered. She was no fan of Little Bluey like Sign used to be, but she certainly didn't think that Little Bluey intentionally left them to freeze. The superhero hadn't even known they were out there.

The doctor turned to look at Signah, grinning knowingly. "You don't think she knew?"

Signah hesitated at that. Was this doctor reading her mind?

"Little Bluey abandoned you in your time of need. She did this to you. It's her fault."

"She should have come," Sign whispered to himself.

But the doctor heard him. "Yes. She should have. But

she did not and you are suffering for it."

Sign would wipe tears flowing down his cheek away, but he no longer had the limbs to do so.

"What would you do if Little Bluey were here now?" the doctor asked. "Would you tell her what you really thought of her?"

"Yes," Sign said.

"Would you show her how angry you are at her?"

"Yes," Sign said again.

What was this doctor playing at? Signah wondered. This was all very unusual. Peculiar even.

"What if you had powers like she did?" the doctor asked, watching Sign closely for his reaction. "Would you show her that there are consequences for her failures?"

"Sign, no," Signah said. "This isn't her fault." She couldn't believe she was defending Little Bluey. Her!

"I would show her," Sign said.

"Would you like the power to show her?" the doctor asked.

Sign did not hesitate. "Yes."

The doctor then shifted her gaze to Signah. "And how about you? What would you do if you could look beautiful again? If you could move again? Feel again? Would you help your brother and show Little Bluey that there are consequences to her actions? Or, in this case, inactions?"

Signah could not believe that this conversation was even real. This doctor was playing some kind of cruel prank on them. But what if she could be whole again? "You could do that?"

"And more," the doctor said, her smile widening.

"Prove it," Signah demanded.

"Challenge accepted," the doctor replied. She then reached out, her arms extending with shiny silver metallic limbs and touched each of them on their chests.

Signah felt a tingle immediately. Something was happening. She did not know who this doctor was. She did not know how this was possible. But in that instant she knew that the doctor's words were true. She and her brother were about to be transformed, healed, enhanced, and clearly trying to confront Little Bluey was the cost of their salvation. She prayed that the price would not be too steep.

CHAPTER

9

What would go down in history as one of the worst winters in New England was slowly, very slowly, coming to an end. It seemed like almost every other day it had snowed again, with no place for the snow to go. Giant mountain-sized mounds could be seen in every parking lot and street intersection. The wind remained so intense that even disturbed and shoveled snow looked smooth and pristine. The trees were all encased in snow and ice, creating a true winter wonderland.

Every time the barrage calmed, people would dig themselves out. Go shopping for more supplies, and try to get back some semblance of normalcy in their routine. Then the weather man would come on the air and warn of another storm to come. The actual snowfall per storm were in no way record breaking—nothing like the Blizzard of 1978—but the frequency of storms and total accumulation definitely made its way into the record books.

A day went by without more snowfall. Then two. Then three. By the fourth day, everyone was hopeful that the worst was behind them. It was a perfect opportunity to go shopping and get some more supplies. Only the supermarkets were pretty bare with all of the people thinking the same thing. Even so, Cary and Ally filled a cart with things that they needed and began heading home again.

The road brought them by the plaza where Ally's old Dance School, Lizzie's Little Dancers, had been. So far no work had been done to try and restore the theatre. It was a shame seeing someplace that Ally had loved so much be in the state that it was. Good memories there to be sure.

"Hi Dance School!" Ally shouted out as they drove by.

Cary replied, sounding almost feminine, "Hi Ally! I miss you!"

"I miss you, too!" Ally replied.

"Keep dancing!"

"I will!" Ally shouted back.

Cary couldn't help but smile. So adorable.

When they got home, Cary helped Ally out of her car

seat and they both went inside. Ally rushed over to see Loveaby.

"Are you okay for a minute?" Cary asked.

"Yup," Ally replied.

"I'm going to unload the car."

He then went back down and made several trips in with the groceries and put them away. After Ally was done playing with Loveaby she came over and helped out.

"What would you like for dinner tonight?" he asked. "What are you in the mood for?"

Ally thought about it for a moment, then said, "Can we have chicken terriyaki?"

"Absolutely," Cary said, leaving a package of the chicken out to begin cooking. "Good choice."

"Can I help?"

"Yeah you can," Cary said. After putting the rest of the groceries away he told her what she needed to do. She got the frying pan out, the pot to make the rice, another one for vegetables, the teriyaki sauce, some extra brown sugar to mix it before adding it on, the cutting board, the PAM cooking spray, and the butter for the rice.

After everything was ready, he told her what to do, one step at a time. He watched closely to make sure she was okay, but he let her do each step. He always believed in the old adage that to learn to cook you had to break a few eggs. He definitely let Ally break a few eggs in her quest to learn.

Every time she did—whether it was an egg or something else that she was learning—he was always very calm, encouraging, and let her know that it was okay.

He still cut the meat himself, but he let her put it into the frying pan and mix it. She was so eager to learn. He loved seeing how happy she was and how excited the simplest things always made her.

When dinner was done, both of them were anxious to try it. "Together," Ally said.

They both took a big bite together, and both said, "Mmmmm." Delicious!

"You're a really good cook," Cary said.

"That's because you taught me," Ally replied.

"But you still did it," Cary pointed out. He took another bite and said, "My compliments to the chef."

As Cary was cleaning the dishes after dinner, the doorbell rang.

"I'll get it," Ally shouted. She ran to the front door and then came back with Heidi in tow. "It's Heidi."

"Hi there," Cary said. "You just missed dinner. Ally cooked."

"It smells wonderful," Heidi said. "Sorry to drop by unannounced. I just needed you to sign something."

"No worries," Cary said. He took a packet of papers that Heidi handed him and looked them over.

"Some permits and things," Heidi said. "Just sign there."

Cary took the pen she was offering and signed the documents. "Here you go."

"Did you hear the news?" Heidi asked as she scanned the documents to make sure they were signed in the right place.

"We haven't been paying attention," Cary said. "Why? What's up? Another storm?"

From the other room, Ally yelled, "Yay! More snow!"

"I hope not. We're running out of places to put it," Cary said.

"Aw," Ally replied, disappointed.

"Not snow. Something calling for Little Bluey."

That caught their attention.

"Excuse me?" Cary asked.

"Did you say Little Bluey?" Ally asked, walking back into the kitchen.

"Something in a rock costume," Heidi explained. "Someone likely looking for their fifteen minutes of fame."

"A costume," Cary said. "Probably something like that."

"Anywho, I need to get this back to legal. I'll see you tomorrow."

"Yeah, tomorrow," Cary said. "Thanks for stopping by. I'll see you out." He walked her to the door and made sure she got into her car without slipping on the snow or ice. As soon as she was driving down the driveway he turned to Ally. "Go turn the television on."

Ally ran into the family room, Cary close behind her. She turned on the television and something that looked like a giant troll made out of rocks and debris was staring right back at her. It was huge, about the size of a small truck, with what looked like massive rocks or boulders for its body and limbs.

"That doesn't look like a costume," Cary said.

"I DARE YOU TO FACE ME!" the creature shouted in a deep, guttural, booming voice.

"Daddy? He wants me?" Ally asked, clearly confused.

"I won't let him hurt you," Cary said, picking her up and holding her in his arms. "Daddy promises."

The screen shifted to Evie Berman, who said, "We remain live with this creature made out of stone who is demanding that our very own superhero, Little Bluey, come to face him. He has informed this reporter that his name is 'Bad Guy.'"

"BAD GUYIE!" the creature shouted to correct her.

"Bad Guyie," Evie Berman corrected. "So far, Bad Guyie has not done anything other than demand Little Bluey's presence. But one must wonder, with a name like that, are the people of Bellingham safe from this monstrosity."

Cary shut the television off. He recognized the shopping plaza where this was being filmed. "Nanny, watch Ally."

"What?" Ally said as Cary set her down.

"Compliance," Nanny said, soaring into the room and hovering by Ally.

"Where are you going?" Ally asked.

"To see just what this creature is," he said. "To see what he really wants."

"We're both superheroes. We're partners. We have to go together."

"Helping out people who are hurt or are in need is one thing, but going to potentially fight some kind of super villain? I'm not going to allow that. I'm not going to risk you getting harmed."

"Daddy, please," Ally pleaded.

"Stay here with Nanny," he said. "I need to know that you're safe."

The tears began welling up in her eyes. He was so torn. He would not take her into potential combat with some unknown super powered individual, but he hated to leave her behind. He gave up being a Protector on his own world to make sure that he was always there for her. Now he was rushing off just like he was still on the job. But what if this Bad Guyie started hurting people if they didn't show up?

"I'll be real careful and I'll come home as soon as I can," he promised. He held her in one last hug, and then got his costume on and was off. There was a potential threat out there. One targeting his daughter. One that had to be dealt with.

CHAPTER 10

Cary recognized the parking lot where Evie Berman was filming. It was the plaza where the movie theater was located. It took him three jumps through the air to land in the lot. He spotted the news van and crews right away by the movies with a giant ten-foot creature that looked like he was made entirely out of stone, asphalt, and other rocky-debris. Based on his time as a Protector, he tried to cross-reference in his mind what that could mean for a power set. He presumed the stone exterior made the body hard, almost shield like. Being hit by stone likely would be a heavy hit, too. Possibly even super strength. Nothing he shouldn't be able to handle on his own.

"This is Evie Berman from WTB TV News reporting to you live from Bellingham where we have been with the monstrous Bad Guyie, who has been demanding that our resident superhero Little Bluey come to face him. This reporter just witnessed none other than Boston Bluey arrive on scene.

"Boston Bluey! Boston Bluey! Do you care to comment on what is happening here? Will Little Bluey be joining you? Do you think this Bad Guyie is some form of genetic evolution or science experiment gone wrong?"

On his world, people knew enough to back off to safety when the Protectorate arrived. Evie Berman and her camera crew were right in the middle of things though. There was also a dozen or so people milled around, trying to see what was happening.

"Everyone, please listen to me, you need to move back to safety until I ascertain what is going on here," Boston Bluey shouted out with as much authority as he could muster. Unfortunately his warning fell on deaf ears.

"WHERE IS LITTLE BLUEY?" the creature shouted in its deep, guttural, booming voice. "WHERE IS SHE?"

"It's past her bedtime, I'm afraid," Boston Bluey said, trying to sound upbeat and defuse the situation. "But I'm here. What can I help you with?"

"I WANT LITTLE BLUEY!" the creature shouted angrily. He took a step toward Boston Bluey, the rocks in his body sounding like they were grinding with the motion, and then the ground tremored slightly when he set his foot down, cratering the parking lot.

"You need to calm down," Boston Bluey advised. "There's nothing to be angry about. And it looks like you're damaging the parking lot. Why don't we just remain calm and discuss what it is that you want."

Bad Guyie took another step, causing another pothole in the pavement, and another tremor. He shouted with anger, "I WANT LITTLE BLUEY!"

"But why?" Boston Bluey asked, bracing himself in anticipation of this confrontation becoming physical.

"SHE ABANDONED ME!"

Boston Bluey did not expect that. How had Ally abandoned this creature? They had never even seen it before. He certainly would remember a ten-foot tall rock creature. Even if Ally had come across this thing without him, which was impossible, there was no way that he would not have heard about it.

"I think you are mistaken," Boston Bluey said. "But we should discuss it. See why you feel that way."

"I HAVE NOTHING TO SAY TO YOU!" he roared.

He then jabbed his fist out as if he were trying to punch

Boston Bluey, but he was too far away to hope to reach the superhero. But then the fist and part of it's arm separated from it's body and came soaring at him. Boston Bluey had little time to react, but dodged to the side. Even so, the fist still clipped him on the left shoulder and sent him spinning backwards three times before he fell to the ground. The stony arm and fist then returned through the air and slammed back onto Bad Guyie with a loud crunch like a wrecking ball slamming through concrete.

Boston Bluey set his hands on the ground and lifted himself up, like a push up, then pushed himself up and sprung to his feet. The pain in his shoulder throbbed. He had enhanced strength and was extremely resistant to harm, but he sure did feel that fist.

"That's a new one," he said to himself. He updated the power profile in his mind. Definitely has super strength, and can control parts of his body. Boston Bluey rubbed his shoulder, then rotated it a couple of times. He kept his gaze on the creature before him, who looked, through the stones that created it's mouth, like he was smiling.

"ARE YOU READY TO BRING ME LITTLE BLUEY NOW?" it asked.

"Yeah, that's going to be a hard no," Boston Bluey said. "And clearly you're not big on diplomacy. So the prover-bial kid gloves are off." He meant for the comment to be intimidating, but Bad Guyie only smiled even wider, show-ing smaller stones for teeth. It was like seeing something out of a Tolkein movie or a nightmare.

"KID GLOVES. CUTE." Bad Guyie said with a deep chuckle. He then ground his fingers into fists, dust flowing off of them as he was squeezing so hard and crushing his own fingers. "BRING IT ON!"

⚡ ⚡ ⚡

"You really should not be watching this," Nanny cau-tioned. "Your father will be fine."

"Look how big it is. Look how scary it is. Did you see how far Daddy got knocked back? He needs my help!" Ally cried.

"Your father left implicit instructions that you were to safely remain out of harm's way."

"But it wants me. What if my being there would end all of this?"

"Or what if you being there got it to attack you?" Nanny countered.

On the television they heard Evie Berman narrating, almost like a sports play-by-play broadcaster. "Boston Bluey has engaged the creature. He has leapt at it and was intercepted, struck down without even coming close to touching it. He's down, but getting up! He is getting up!"

Ally gasped. "My Daddy needs me!" She reached for her pendant, ready to activate her costume, but Nanny stopped her.

"You must remain here. Your father would deactivate me for sure if I allowed you to go."

Ally returned her gaze to the television. "Get up, Daddy! Get up!"

N N N

Ow, ow, ow. That didn't work. Boston Bluey had leapt at Bad Guyie, intending to deliver an uppercut punch to its rocky chin. But before he even got there one of the fists slammed down on him from above while in mid-flight. That hurt. That will still hurt tomorrow morning. A lot.

"GIVE UP, HERO," Bad Guyie said, chuckling again. "IT'S MY TIME NOW. YOU AND LITTLE BLUEY ARE YESTERDAY'S NEWS."

Boston Bluey heard the sirens. More police had arrived. Hopefully they could get the civilians out of the way. He also hoped that they did not try to engage this thing. If he couldn't hit it, he suspected that bullets would just bounce off.

His back was throbbing, joining his shoulder with pain.

But he fought through it, forcing himself up. He could not recall the last time he felt pain like this. Even fighting criminals on his own world. Being strong and nearly invulnerable brought a certain sense of security that you couldn't be hurt. Clearly that wasn't true.

"HUNGRY FOR MORE?"

Boston Bluey tried to sound stronger and with more bravado than he felt at the moment. "If you can dish it, I can take it. Now stand down before someone gets hurt."

"LIKE YOU!" Bad Guyie said as he went to punch Boston Bluey.

Boston Bluey was prepared this time. He had seen the rocky fists separate from the creature's body. He had felt the impact twice. As the fist came at him, he used his own strength and caught the fist. He then channeled his power through his own body to send the creature off balance and toss him to the side.

The most peculiar thing happened. As Bad Guyie was separated from the ground, even though it was only for a few seconds, he had grown smaller, some of the larger rocks and debris falling from him and his body shrinking down in size. As soon as he landed on the ground though, the stones went back and he returned to the size he was.

Curious. Boston Bluey thought. This creature somehow was using cohesion to draw the rocks and debris to him.

But when he was not touching the ground, he wound up losing cohesion. He might be able to beat this thing if he could keep it from touching the ground and then knocking him out before he reformed. That was a big "might" though.

Bad Guyie stood back up and turned upon him, glaring at him. "THAT TICKLED."

A loud speaker blared over the parking lot, drawing both of their attention. "This is the police! Cease and desist immediately! This is your only warning!"

"You should listen to them," Boston Bluey said.

"NOT LIKELY," Bad Guyie said as he raised both arms and his fingers shot out at the police cars, forcing the officers to dive down for cover.

"No!" Boston Bluey shouted. He then used one of his most powerful abilities. He leapt into the air and channeled the electrical currents that flowed through him down into his foot. He then struck Bad Guyie in the back, trying to divert its attention from the police officers, and shouted, "Power kick!" As he struck, all of the momentum of the jump, all of his strength channeled into his kick, all of his electrical current surging through his foot, released in a devastating blow upon his foe.

Bad Guyie fell face first to the ground, landing hard and causing a major tremor with the impact. Boston Bluey landed atop of him, looking for a way to either keep the creature down or get it in the air to test out his hypothesis on needing to touch the ground to maintain cohesion. But it wasn't Bad Guyie who moved next. Boston Bluey was struck from behind by something else.

He fell to the ground and slid all the way to the police cars before being able to turn around and look at what hit him. There was a girl there. She was garbed in a blend of purple and black colors, looking like some kind of blend between medieval sorceress and goth. Her hair was a shimmering and shiny pink, like something out of a cartoon, and her face was painted purple and had glitter on it.

"Who are you?" Boston Bluey asked as he took her appearance in.

"You don't know me yet. But you will," she said, grinning devilishly. She then clasped a crystal that she was wearing around her neck, and a portal opened beneath both her and Bad Guyie and they simply lowered into the ground and then vanished.

Once they were gone, the entire parking lot was eerily quiet. Boston Bluey slowly got up, feeling all of the aches and pains from the encounter, and he looked at the police officers. "Is everyone okay?"

"What were those things?" one asked.

"I don't know," Boston Bluey admitted. "But I'm going

to find out."

Evie Berman came running over with her camera man. "Boston Bluey! Boston Bluey! A moment of your time, please! Our viewers wish to know where these two came from. Are they here just because of you, or would they have come anyway?"

"Excuse me?" Boston Bluey asked.

"While real life superheroes may be knew, the theme of superheroes is not. It has been a longstanding belief in superhero lore that the mere presence of the hero leads to those who are determined to beat them. In essence, the hero creates the villain instead of merely trying to help those in need. Has your recent appearance here resulted in this? Are these villains here because you are? Has your presence alone created these fiends?"

That was a loaded question to be sure. He had no answer. He had no clue who these two were, why they were here, what they wanted with Little Bluey, or where they came from. But the way the reporter was asking the question, he suspected quite a few people would begin to turn on them, blaming them for the sudden appearance of these new villains.

He did his best to defuse the situation. "At this time I do not care to speculate as to the origins or motivations of the two we just encountered. Clearly we need more information as anything we say would be pure guesswork. In time, I trust we will learn who they are and what they really want. Thank you."

Evie Berman tried to ask a follow-up question, but Boston Bluey crouched down and then leapt up into the air and far from the movie theater parking lot. There was nothing further to be gained here this day, and it was a slippery slope when dealing with public perception.

Three jumps and he was back home.

"Daddy!" a tear-flowing Ally shouted as she ran and leapt into his arms. "Daddy, I was so worried! Are you okay?"

"I'm okay, I'm okay," he said. "I'm so sorry you had to experience that. Had to see it. But I'm okay." At least this time. Finding out who Bad Guyie and the girl with him were just became his top priority. They wanted Ally, and he had to do whatever it took to protect his little princess.

CHAPTER

11

Getting Ally to fall asleep that night was understandably difficult. She did not want to be away from her father at all and felt the need to cuddle and hold him close. He was always so protective of her, but he knew she felt the same way in return. It was the two of them against the world. Nothing bad could happen to either of them. They were all that each other had in life.

When Ally did finally fall asleep in his arms, her head on his shoulder, Cary very slowly, so that he would not wake her up, reached over to the end table by the bed and got ahold of his communicator. He slipped it into his ear and whispered, "Nanny?"

The voice of Nanny came back over the comm system. He had to be quiet so as not to wake Ally up, but Nanny's voice was right inside his ear and would not bother Ally at all.

"Nanny, open a file on the two enhanced individuals I encountered today. Name one 'Bad Guyie' and the other 'Unknown Female.'"

"Compliance," Nanny replied. "Proceed."

"Transfer all appropriate visual images into each file. For Bad Guyie, take note, strong, ability to control limbs beyond the connection to his body, armor-like. His steps had concussive force, making tremors that shook the ground and damaged the pavement beneath him. The impacts of his strikes are powerful enough to hurt me. Possible weakness noted when he was not physically touching the ground. Something we might be able to exploit in the future. Clear obsession with Little Bluey, but the reason why remains unknown.

"For Unknown Female, take note, she struck me behind with some kind of force blast that cascaded through my body and made me feel like my nerves were on fire. She also has some form of teleportation ability that extends beyond just herself as she transported Bad Guyie as well. Also make a note that before she transported she touched her necklace. It's possible that the necklace is some kind of device with powers and it is not coming from her at all."

Cary paused at that. Did these two have enhanced abilities, or was it some kind of artificial enhancement? "Add to both files a query as to try and determine their origins and source of their abilities."

"Compliance," Nanny replied.

"Monitor all news and social media outlets for any reference of these two, flag it, and add appropriate data to the file."

"Compliance."

"Also, conduct a global search for any and all references of enhanced beings. Ally and I found plenty of references in pop culture, movies, television, comics, books, toys, and the like. But are there reported cases of individuals with abilities on this world? Access government databases as well, especially any redacted files that you may be able to uncover."

"What are you hoping to find?" Nanny inquired.

"I want to know if we're really alone on this world, or if there are others with enhanced abilities. If there are others, how did they get their powers? Are they from this world or is it possible that they are from ours? It might also help determine the source of Bad Guyie and Unknown Female's abilities."

"Understood."

"Oh, and Nanny, this should go without saying, but don't get caught. We don't want the governments of the world coming after us for accessing their files."

"Please," Nanny said in what sounded like robotic-sarcasm. "The systems on this world are quite primitive. I will find what you are seeking without anyone being any the wiser."

"Thank you," Cary said. "That will be all for tonight."

"Good night, sir."

Cary took the communicator out of his ear and slowly moved his arm to put it on the end table. Ally did not stir at all, though her breathing was erratic and she whimpered a few times. She was having a bad dream. He kissed her on the forehead, held her tight, and gently caressed her arm. "Daddy has you. You're okay. Daddy has you," he said, trying to be reassuring. She stopped whimpering and re-mained asleep the rest of the night.

CHAPTER

12

When Ally woke up in the morning, she was just as tender and cuddly as the night before. She did not want to be out of sight of her Daddy, and more than that, wanted him to pick her up and carry her everywhere. She would just stop in her tracks, raise her arms, and say, "Pick me up."

"Absolutely," he would reply, even if his arms were full. He could make a couple of trips if need be. Right now she needed him close, the comfort, the realization that he was there and that everything was and would be okay.

He was very sore though. Where Bad Guyie had punched him was red and swollen and tender to the touch.

Even when Ally hugged him tight and it sent ripples of pain through him, he just smiled and bore it, not wanting her to know that he had actually gotten hurt as bad as he had.

"How about you feed Loveaby?" Cary asked.

"I don't want to leave you," Ally whimpered, holding him even tighter.

"I'm right here, I'm not going anywhere," he said reassuringly.

"Okay, I'll feed her," she reluctantly said.

He set her down and watched as she slowly inched away from him to get the food for her pet dragon. Once she had the cabinet open where the pet food was, he shifted his attention to getting breakfast ready. He poured them each a glass or orange juice—Ally's in an adorable *The Little Mermaid* cup that was see-through blue and looked like it was water—and got their vitamins ready.

"Hot chocolate?" he asked.

"Yeah," she replied as she filled Loveaby's bowl with dog food. For a dragon, Loveaby sure did love the dog food on this world.

Cary filled the kettle and put it on the stove, turning it on. He then debated what he should make for breakfast. He usually asked Ally what she was in the mood for, but she needed some smiles this morning. He knew... Mickey Mouse pancakes!

When Ally was done with Loveaby, Cary said, "Want to help me with breakfast?"

"Yes!" she said.

"Can you get the pink mixing bowl out?"

Ally went right to the cabinet where the mixing bowls were. The pink one was in a set of four different colored bowls, each a different size. The pink one he always thought was perfect for mixing pancake mix or when baking cookies or brownies. She got the bowl out and handed it to him.

"Now can you get the pancake mix from the cabinet?" he asked. He watched as she lifted off of the ground, hovered over the counter and opened the cabinet, removing the pancake mix. She already seemed like she was doing better with her mind on something other than what happened last night.

"Here you go, Daddy," she said as she lowered herself back down to the floor and set the pancake mix on the counter.

"Now get the measuring cups."

She went right to the proper drawer and took the measuring cups out.

"How hungry are you today?" he asked.

"Very hungry," she replied.

"Okay, then pour two cups of mix into the bowl."

Even though she could fly, when she was cooking in the kitchen they had a green folding chair that she used. She got it and moved it over and climbed up on it. "Two cups?"

"Two cups."

Ally poured the mix into the measuring cup. Some overflowed and she looked up at him. "Uh oh."

"It's okay," he replied. "You're still learning. You're doing great."

She then went back at it, pouring the first cup into the mixing bowl and then filling a second cup, this time without spilling. It amazed him to see how she was developing. She could make custom-made bow and arrows, but still managed to spill a little pancake mix. He was glad for that. He was in no rush for her to grow up too soon. He'd miss having his Ally when she was this young.

"I love you," he said.

She paused mid-pour of the second cup of pancake mix into the bowl and looked over at him. Her face lit up, her smile infectious. "I love you more."

"If you think so," Cary teased.

"I love you more than anybody else loves you."

Cary thought about that for a moment. "You know, that's probably true. Though I bet if we could talk to Grandma she'd debate you on that."

"I wish we could call Grandma," Ally said.

Yeah, that would be nice, but a little hard to manage since she was in another reality. To the best of his knowledge, there was no such thing as an inter-dimensional telephone.

"Hopefully we'll see her again one day," Cary said. He then directed Ally through the rest of the pancakes. This particular box that they had bought was a "just add water" box, so it was pretty simple to make them. "Stir it real good."

"Okay," she said.

"Count to..." he paused, thinking about a number that might be challenging for her. She was doing tens now, but sometimes struggled with the numbers in between. "Fifty-eight."

"Fifty-eight?" she asked.

"Fifty-eight," he repeated.

She began counting as the kettle began to whistle. He prepared their mugs of hot chocolate while she continued to stir. This time he picked out Disney Princesses Snow White and Aurora for the mugs. He tilted them towards Ally. "Which one did you want?"

She kept counting, but inserted her answer. "Eighteen, nineteen, Aurora, twenty."

He finished making their hot chocolates. For Ally's he always added some cold milk to it so that it was not too hot and wouldn't burn her mouth. His mother used to boil the milk for him in a pan when she made Hot Chocolate or tea. As Ally got older he'd probably start doing that so she could still have mostly milk in her mug, but for now he just wanted her drink to be warm instead of scalding.

"Thirty, forty," she said.

"What was that?" he gently corrected.

"I meant, thirty-one, thirty-two," she said, continuing on.

"Very good," he commended her. When she reached fifty-eight, he said, "Let's see how it looks."

She leaned back to show him the bowl, lifting her spatula and showing the pancake mix dripping off. "How's it look?"

"Perfect," he said, smiling widely.

He then pulled out the electric fryer, which was long enough to make two rows of three normal sized pancakes at a time, or two big Mickey Mouse pancakes. He turned it on to preheat it.

"How about getting us some fruit," he said.

Ally got down from the green chair and walked over to the refrigerator. She opened it up and looked at their options. She came back with a bowl of strawberries. He had never liked the taste of strawberries, but Ally loved them.

"Good pick, my dear," he said.

"Why thank you," she replied with a pretend curtsey.

"I'll do this part," he said. "Can you go set the table?"

"Okay," she replied and was off on her next task.

He turned on the sink and dabbed a little water on his fingers. He flicked it at the frying pan and saw the water turn into little balls and dance along the top before evaporating. It was the sign that the temperature was just right. He then got the ladle and very carefully poured the batter onto the grill—one big round pancake and two smaller ones at the top for ears for each of them.

With the batter on the frying pan, he took out a cutting board and knife and cut the strawberries up. In the middle of doing so it was time to flip the pancakes. He then finished with the strawberries and got the plates down. He did Ally's first, and arranged the cut up strawberries to look like eyes, a nose, and a mouth.

"Order up," he said, acting like they were in a restaurant. He got the pancake syrup out of the cabinet and brought that and the two plates of food over to where Ally had set up their tables. He made a second trip to get the mugs of hot chocolate. When everything was on the table, he asked, "Do you need anything else?"

"I'm good," she said.

"Do you want to cut it or do you want me to do it?"

Sometimes she would try to do it herself, and if she had trouble she would ask for help. That's what he expected this morning, especially with the Mickey Mouse pancakes, but she immediately said, "You do it."

"I'd be delighted. Do you want the syrup on first or are you going to dip?"

"First please."

"Sure thing." He poured the syrup over the Mickey Mouse pancakes, let her take one last look at the cute little face on the plate looking up at her, and then he cut it up for her. "Here you go."

"Thank you, Daddy."

"Anytime," he replied as he picked the syrup back up and put it onto his pancakes.

The two ate their breakfast, and while he knew she was still concerned about the prior night, it was a new day with new things to do, and he was glad to see that she was moving on and not acting as worried as she had been. She definitely stayed close and cuddly to him all day, but things were getting back to normal. For now. But the threat was still out there, and he knew he had to deal with it and make sure Ally was never put in danger. Nanny was working on her assignment, and that would be a concern for another day. Today was all about love, comfort, and reassurance.

CHAPTER
13

Somewhere else, but closer than any of them would know, Sign and Signah returned to their own home. They were never officially released from the hospital, but instead left with the doctor who had been full of promises. They did not remember much after that. They each had glimpses and memories of being on stretchers, and seeing bright lights, but then nothing. When they woke up, the doctor was gone, and they had powers.

Sign was lying in a bed of rocks, and as he tried to move, the rocks all responded to him, merging with him. He suddenly had limbs again and could move. It had been cumbersome at first, but he got the hang of it quickly.

Signah did not feel any differently than she had before she had been trapped in the snow. She could move freely again and was without pain. She found a mirror and looked inside of it and she appeared just like she always had before the storm. But the moment she touched her favorite crystal, her whole body pulsated with power and emitted a purple aura around her. She heard a voice in her mind, as if the crystal was talking to her, teaching her just what she was now capable of doing.

They each chose their new names. Sign wanted to be Bad Guyie. Signah decided to go with Crystal. With the doctor gone, they had little guidance or direction, but they vividly recalled the deal. They were transformed, healed in a way, and the price of this miracle was going after Little Bluey.

Signah still had doubts and did not want to do so. It wasn't Little Bluey's fault what happened to them. But Sign was adamant. He went to try and draw her out. Signah went along to keep an eye on him, but was more reluctant and tried to stay in the background. Until she saw that her brother was in trouble and needed her.

He had done well against Boston Bluey. More than held his own. He really seemed to hurt the elder hero. But like most heroes do in the movies, they kept fighting even on the brink of defeat and found a way. Boston Bluey found a way. But he did not know that Sign was not alone. He wouldn't make that mistake a second time. If there was a second time.

"WHY DIDN'T SHE COME?" Sign demanded, still covered by rocks.

"You'll wake Mom," Signah said.

The rocks flowed off of Sign and landed in a pile, making a chair for him to sit on. He spoke normally when the rocks were not covering his body. "Why didn't she come? She was supposed to come!"

"You got Boston Bluey. That's a good start, right?"

"It's Little Bluey I want!" Sign shouted. "She's the one who left me."

"Sign, it's not like that. You know that." She still couldn't believe she was the one defending Little Bluey now. Why not embrace the super villain role like her brother had? But did she really see herself as a villain? Did she want to be a villain?

Their mother stumbled into the room, looking like she just woke up. "What's all of this racket? Some people are trying to sleep!"

"Sorry Mom," Signah said.

Their mother started to leave, but then stood there looking very confused. "When did you get home?"

112

"Just now," Signah said.

"They let you out of the hospital without calling me to pick you up?" she asked. "Why I have a mind to file a complaint! My kids on their own. They are going to hear about this."

She then walked away and left the siblings alone.

"Are we going to get in trouble for leaving the hospital?" Sign asked.

Signah winced. The hospital was probably looking for them. They would think that they were kidnapped or ran away. This wasn't good. "We need to go back."

"I don't want to go back," Sign said.

"Mom will get in trouble because of us," Signah said.

"How?" Sign wanted to know.

"They'll think she brought us home without being released by the hospital. We have to go back."

"But I need to find Little Bluey."

"We'll worry about that later. For now, we're going back."

Sign was clearly not happy, but said, "Fine."

Signah touched her crystal and a portal opened up beneath them. They sunk into the portal, like quicksand, and emerged back in their bed.

A nurse ran into the room, looking frantic and unsettled. "You're here? You weren't here a minute ago!"

"Sorry, we went for a walk," Signah said.

The nurse looked confused. Who could blame her? The paralyzed girl and her amputee brother had suddenly gone for a walk? Good luck figuring out how that happened.

N N N

Sign and Signah's mother walked back into their room. "Are you hungry?" She looked from side to side and did not see her children. "Sign? Signah?" she waited, then rubbed her eyes. "I must be more tired than I thought. I'm hallucinating now."

CHAPTER

14

Surprisingly, there was no follow-up encounter with Bad Guyie and the Unknown Female. Not that Cary was complaining, but he knew deep down that this was far from over and that troubled him. Still, life got back to normal, or for what passed as normal on this world.

The media still kept discussing what happened and asking people for their thoughts. Some people were fascinated by people with abilities. Some people were terrified. Some had confidence that Boston Bluey would, and this was a direct quote, "Kick that rock-dude's rocky-butt!" Others seemed to wish that Boston and Little Bluey had never come to their little town. But overall, Cary got the sense that most people were still viewing he and Ally favorably, so, they did begin patrolling and helping people again.

Their patrols were not against supervillains, but they helped a little old lady with a walker cross the road. They saved a bus of Elementary School children who had gotten stuck in the mud and their tires were just spinning. They even helped one family recover a trampoline that had blown away in one of the storms and then had been covered by snow. It was nice helping people again, and even more so that Ally could get out and feel like a superhero again.

But life was also getting busier. The Dance Recital was quickly coming upon them and was scheduled for Father's Day weekend. There were costume fittings, and specific makeup that needed to be acquired, and tap shoes that needed to be spray painted to match the costumes—rather than having to buy new ones just for the recital, and pictures that needed to be scheduled and taken, and hair that needed to be done.

Ally was going to have two dances at the recital, one for tap and one for jazz. Her tap outfit was black and white. She was dressed like a sequined penguin, with a tuxedo front full of bow tie and cummerbund, and a feathered take with fishnet stalking. She also had a small top hat that was

116

work at a slant on the side of her head. The outfit was adorable and she loved the feathers.

The first night at Dance School when they got to try on their outfits, the entire class came marching out in costume so that the parents in the waiting area could see them. Ally was all smiles, so excited, so happy.

For Jazz, they let the parents into the studio to help their kids change from one costume to the other. Her jazz outfit was lime green and white and full of sparkles. There was a lime green long sleeved leotard, a white cotton vest with sparkly lime green shoulders, and a blend of green and white on a tutu. Ally adored her tutu, so much she wanted to know if she could add a tutu to her superhero costume. Anything is possible! The jazz outfit was finished off with a sparkly lime green bow for her hair that was worn right in front of her hair bun.

At the recital, they would switch outfits between dances, and again for the final number. For the finale they would all wear their own dresses and with a t-shirt over it with the Awgle Dance and Gymnastics Academy name and logo on it. As was becoming customary, single Daddy's had a hard time at recitals since he wasn't allowed to go into the back to help Ally change. There really should be a room designated for people in their situation. Fortunately, he had made good friends with some of the mothers who were also

117

at the same Dance School and they offered to help out.

The end of June also brought Ally's birthday. She was going to be turning five soon! This year she decided that she wanted a PAW Patrol birthday party. Cary went out and bought banners and balloons of the pups—including one big balloon that played the PAW Patrol theme song when you hit it. He also got some of the toys to use as centerpieces on the table, like the Lookout, the home base of the PAW Patrol. He then got a little inventive and tried to create themes and made signs and displays, like Captain Turbot's Catch of the Day for shrimp cocktail, or Farmer Yummi's Farm Stand for the fruit and vegetable platters, or Farmer Al's Dairy Barn for the cheese and crackers, or Katie's Puptacular Pup Treats for an assortment of candies and fruit snacks and chips, or Mayor Goodway's Very Good Drinks for the lemonade stand, or Mr. Porter's Pizza for the food. Ally helped with the names and they printed out colored pictures of the characters and made signs to set up for everything.

Cary also found giant PAW Patrol letters that had color themed with the pups, like "A" had Everest on it, or Skye, or Chase. He went through searching for the letters and made several printouts of them to spell out her name, each time without duplicating a character in her name. He brought these to Dance School and worked on cutting them out while Ally was dancing. But when he was done, he hung them up several places throughout the house, along with PAW Patrol posters and several themed banners. There was even a full-wall mural of the pups that went into their family room. There was also little decorations and streamers and images of the pups hanging from the ceiling, some standees and symbols from the show on display around the house, new themed table mats, themed cups and plates, and with the show on in the background.

He had fun gathering everything and ordering the extra special cake for Ally. Birthdays were a big festive occasion, especially when you were turning five! He then created a special invitation, blending together images of the PAW Patrol and a picture of Ally and the details of the party. He debated whether the party should be her actual birthday weekend, or the weekend before the recital, and decided on before the recital. After the recital, too many of her friends might already be on vacation. So this would work out well. Ally brought in invitations and handed them out to each of her friends at dance school in all three of her classes—tap, jazz, and gymnastics. Cary had spoked to the owner to make sure she had the right number of girls so that Ally didn't miss anyone and make them feel left out.

They also invited friends from their original Dance School, and a few of the people that they had become friendly with, like Heidi. Cary hoped that it would be a good turnout for her. But that was still something for another time. Now, it was time for their recital pictures!

Cary had scheduled time with a local photographer, Mindy Shaw Photography, and she was going to take pictures of Ally in each outfit. Cary got dressed in black pants, a lime green shirt, and tie as well, hoping to get a picture of the two of them. He imagined hanging a three-framed picture with them in the middle and then Ally on each side in her two costumes.

According to the GPS in Flowers, their Chevrolet Trax, it would take them just under fifteen minutes to get to the photography studio. Cary carefully loaded up both of the outfits in travel suitcases to make sure they did not get dirty or damaged. He brought Ally's normal Disney Princess dance bag that had a change of tights in case one got a snag so he could change them for the pictures, and it also had her shoes. He also had a bag of hair products—even though he had already done Ally's hair at home, he still had a brush, a comb, more hair ties, more hair pins, a blonde hair net, hair gel, hair spray, and even a toothbrush just in case he needed to brush in some tiny strands of hair. Like her hair, Cary also did Ally's makeup before they left. He took the makeup supplies with him, too, just in case she needed a touch up with the blush, eye shadow, mascara, or lipstick.

"I think we are good to go," Cary said. "Are you ready?"

Ally made her way down the stairs and over to the car. "I'm ready."

"Are you excited?"

Ally nodded her head excitedly. She loved dancing so much, and getting her pictures taken professionally to hang on the wall was something that she had been looking forward to. Cary was glad for the pictures, too. The memories. He tried to take a lot of pictures and also write letters to Ally that he intended to give her when she graduated from college. His "Letters to Ally," which chronicled their lives and memories together, with pictures embedded, so one day she could look back and see all of the amazing things that they had done and remember things that most children would forget about.

They arrived a few minutes before their appointment and headed inside. It was a big building, a former mill that had been refurbished for businesses, like Mindy Shaw Photography. Everything was quite lovely from the front foyer to the decorations in the long hallways.

"This is it," Cary said, seeing the door that said Mindy Shaw Photography.

He knocked and heard someone shout, "It's open," from inside.

Cary opened the door and Ally went inside first. It was a big studio, with a very comfortable looking couch, chairs, and pillows. All of the décor was white. Hanging on the walls were blown up pictures of past clients.

"Come in, come in, this must be Ally," the woman, Mindy, said. She was all smiles and very pleasant and Ally took to her immediately. "I hear someone is about to have their dance recital."

"I am," Ally said, a cross between shy and excitement.

"You must be looking forward to it."

"She most definitely is," Cary said.

Ally nodded enthusiastically.

"How many dances are you going to do?" Mindy asked.

"Two," Ally replied.

"Two dances? That's great!" She then looked up at Cary. "You said you wanted pictures in each outfit?"

"Yes," Cary said holding the suitcase up to show that he had the outfits. "And one of the both of us together would be great."

"Perfect. Why don't you get her changed and we'll get started? Can I get either of you anything? A drink?"

"I'm good, thank you. Ally?"

"No thank you," Ally said.

"Want to start with the black or green outfit?" Cary asked.

Ally thought about it for a moment, and then said, "Green."

"Perfect," Cary replied. That probably was the better pick. The hat for the black outfit he felt had a better chance of messing up her hair, so this worked out well.

Cary helped Ally change into her costume. The Dance School really did do an amazing job of picking out adorable outfits. Ally most definitely was adorable.

Mindy was standing next to a table by the section she had set up for the photoshoot. She looked up as they walked over. "All set?"

"We are," Cary said.

"Right this way," Mindy said, leading Ally over to part of the studio with massive lights shining down and a white background. She had props, like stools or small chairs or love seats to sit on, but she explained that for the typical dance picture she didn't use these, having the kids stand and really show off their outfits. She took a few pictures and then had Ally shift her position and stand different ways. Every now and again she would say, "Perfect," or "Just like that," or "You're doing great."

When Mindy was done with the pictures of the first outfit, Ally said, "With Daddy."

"Go get in there," Mindy said.

Cary walked over and got into the picture. Ally looked

right at him and smiled. He smiled back, their noses practically touching. Cary noticed that Mindy was already snapping pictures.

"Do you want us to get in some kind of pose?" Cary asked.

"That was cute," she said. "Just keep doing what you're doing."

But Ally said, "Pick me up."

Cary picked her up into his arms and Mindy took a few more pictures. This time she did offer some instructions, about looking at her and smiling.

"I think we go it," she said. "Why don't you change outfits."

Cary helped Ally again, being very careful as they took each item off and packing it safely and securely for the next time they needed it at the dress rehearsal. They then changed into the new costume, the black penguin tuxedo with feathered tails fishnet stockings, and the little top hat tilted on the side of her head.

As they went back for the last round of pictures though, Ally adamantly said, "With Daddy."

"Honey, we did the pictures of us. This is you in this outfit."

"With you," she said again, determined to have pictures of the two of them.

"Go ahead," Mindy said. She then snapped a few pictures of the two of them. "Your turn now."

Ally let her Daddy go off to the side and watch and began the last photoshoot of the day. But after taking a few pictures, she was pretty much done with pictures for the day.

"Can I just get one more shot?" Mindy asked, trying to direct Ally to do what she wanted for the final pose.

"I want a picture like this," Ally said as she jumped up in the air and spread her arms and legs before coming back down to a landing.

"Do you want to do your pose and then mine?" Mindy asked, trying to negotiate.

"Just this," Ally said, jumping up in the air again.

"I think she's pretty much done," Cary said. "Try the pose she wants, that should be good enough. We got quite a few."

Ally smiled wide at that and jumped up and down a few more times as Mindy snapped some more pictures.

"And done," Mindy said. "You can get changed now."

"Yay!" Ally shouted.

Just like with the first outfit, Cary was very careful about taking the outfit off and putting it away. Then he got Ally back in her original outfit.

"So what's next?" Cary asked.

"I'll email you a link and password to access the photos of the shoot after I work my magic on them. Then you just need to let me know which ones you want."

"Sounds good, thank you.".

"Thanks for coming in," Mindy said. "Ally, it was lovely meeting you."

"I was lovely meeting you, too," Ally replied.

⚡ ⚡ ⚡

It took a few days before the email came with the link. As soon as Cary saw it, he called for Ally to join him so that they could look and pick out the pictures together. They selected one of Ally in each outfit, and one of both of them in each of Ally's outfits. Instead of a 3-windowed frame, they looked online and ordered two separate 2-picture frames and would put a single picture of Ally and a picture of both of them next to it. They also took the picture Ally wanted of her jumping and ordered a separate frame for that one, which would go in Daddy's office so he could always see it and remember the moment.

CHAPTER

15

As the birthday party got closer and closer, Cary begin to grow a little concerned that Ally would not have any friends who came to it. Nobody had responded to the little invitations that they handed out at Dance School. If it was just the two of them, he would make sure she had so much fun, but he knew how excited she was to have friends come over and did not want to disappoint. So he printed out the invitations a second time and put a big "Reminder" banner on it and had her hand them out again.

Fortunately, this time, he got some replies. Lizzie said that she and Tanya would be there. Ally's new best friend at Dance School was Kaitlyn, and her mother sat near Cary in the waiting room and they were social. With the reminder they said that they were coming. The other mother who Cary sat with had a daughter, Riley, in with Ally, and twins, Chloe and Zoey, who were in the waiting room with her—they both went to Dance School, too, but were a year younger and danced a different night. All three were in.

When class had ended, one of the other mothers, mother of Lyla, crouched down next to Ally and said, "Hey sweetie, Lyla is going to come to your birthday party. What did you want?"

Ally thought about it for a moment, smiled, and said, "A PAW Patrol blanket."

"You got it," she said. "We'll see you there."

Six girls, plus Ally. Cary was so relieved that they got a response and he knew who was coming. It also helped with planning the food. For the "Mr. Porter's Pizzas," he made signs to attach to the pizza boxes so that it looked like it had come from Mr. Porter's restaurant in Adventure Bay of PAW Patrol. It also helped him know how many grab bags to get, how much food and drink, and the plates and silverware.

With the last few details finalized, he and Ally went shopping to get the final things, and then began setting up the displays that they had been creating. The various stations and corresponding decorations were all set up, the food was ready to go, the cake—which was round and full of sparkles and had Skye from PAW Patrol on the top, along with a box of matching decorated cupcakes—was made by one of the neighbors who had her own pastry business on the side, Loveaby and Nanny were hidden away so as not to draw any attention to them, and it was time to get dressed.

Cary had bought Ally a new dress for her birthday. It was white and blue striped with a pink ribbon around her waist like a belt tying into a big bow. He was debating between the headband or white lace bow, but Ally did not want anything, so they left it long and loose. She did add a necklace that they found while getting the party favors that was a heart and had the number five in the middle for her age.

Heidi was the first to arrive, and she brought her dog Everest with her. Ally rushed over to the door and opened it up to greet her.

"Hi there," Heidi said.

"Come on in," Ally replied, all smiles. This was her special day and she intended to love every moment of it.

Heidi came inside and Cary welcomed her, too. "Welcome. Do you want the quick tour?"

"I'll show you," Ally said. She took Heidi by the hand and led her inside, showing off all of the decorations and displays and where the food was. Everest was the first to eat, with Ally giving her a carrot from Farmer Yumi's Farm Stand display—which came complete with a checkered table cloth and the food in a wicker basket.

After Heidi was settled, Ally went back to the door and peered out the window for her friends. It wasn't long before the next car arrived and parked on the street. "Someone is here!" she shouted.

Cary came to look and saw that it was Lyla and her mother. Just as with Heidi, Ally opened the door and welcomed them in.

"Am I early?" Lyla's mother asked.

Cary glanced at the clock. The invitations said that the party had begun fifteen minutes earlier. "Earlier than everyone else, but good."

"I was going to say, we're never early."

A couple of cars arrived at the same time, and Kaitlyn came running up to the front door shouting, "Ally! Ally! Ally!" the entire way. Both of her parents were walking up behind her. A van had also arrived with Riley, her sisters, and their mother. By the time they made it to the door, Ms. Lizzie and Tanya had arrived.

After Ally greeted everyone and welcomed them in, Ally asked, "Who would like the detour?"

Cary interjected as he saw a few questioning looks at the

word 'detour.' "She wants to give a *tour* of the house. Who wants to see the house?"

Usually Ally would go around from room to room. She may say, "You tell it," to prompt Cary to tell the story of building the house and strange things that happened with the Builder and suppliers, like the big confusion over the closet in the front hall—his Realtor had called up and said that the builder wanted to know if he wanted a closet in the front hall. Cary responded with, what he felt was, a reasonable question: "How much?" The selling Realtor responded, "In the front hall." To which Cary replied again, "Yes, but how much?" This time he got a copy of the floorplan and a circle where the closet would go. Again, Cary asked, "How much?" The same floorplan came back, this time the circle was highlighted, and a comment of, "Does he not understand where it will go?" was added. Cary replied again, "I understand where the closet would go. But how much to put it there?" Then he finally got a response... "Free. A gift from the builder." Well, in that case, yes!—or over the lighting—when Cary asked about the light fixtures and what was included and how did that work, the selling realtor ignored his question and said, "Look at this beautiful molding. The builder doesn't have to do that, but does that special to make the walls look nice." Right, beautiful... but what does that have to do with light fixtures?—or the granite selection—when Cary had first driven into the granite suppliers lot, he saw a slab that he instantly fell in love with. But they had five slabs to show him that he could pick from. He asked how much more would it be to get the one he wanted, to which they replied, "You don't want that, that would be extra." He understood that, but how much extra. After going back and forth and being told multiple times that he did not want that, they finally told him it would be an extra $15 per square foot. So what were they arguing for? Do it!

This time though, she just told her friends to follow her and rushed upstairs to show them her rooms and so that they could all play together. Cary then gave the full tour to the parents, including the stories and showing each room and talking about the decisions that they had made, like with the dining room set, or making the basement ceiling higher, or putting plywood down in the space beyond the walk-in closet instead of particle board so that exercise equipment could go there and he'd be more confident that it was safe.

When the tour made it to the pink room, or rather the room that he and Ally painted pink to match one of her sweaters that she loved, they found all of the kids playing together.

"We'll be downstairs if you need anything," Cary said.

"Okay," Ally replied.

When the parents were all back downstairs, they began chatting and having a good time together, too, sampling on the food and snacks out for the party. Lyla's mother said, while looking at all of the decorations, "You really go all out."

"Yeah, I try to be creative. It gives us a little project to work on together, and we have fun with it."

"Lyla would be lucky if we had just a 'Happy Birthday' banner."

"I know, right?" Kaitlyn's mother said, laughing to herself.

The girls stayed upstairs for a while, then made their way down to the rest of the party. Ally walked up to her Daddy and asked, "Can we paint?"

That definitely had not been part of the plan. When Ally painted, he always put one of his sleeveless exercise shirts over her as her paint shirt to protect her from getting dirty. But with other kids, he didn't want to treat her differently. They could all really make a mess with the paints, but at least the paints they had were washable.

"If you use the bench outside and everyone gets permission from their parents first," Cary decided. The bench was set up under a pop-up gazebo and had balloons on every chair. There were also other lawn chairs and small end tables scattered throughout the yard, plus the sandbox, swing set, and trampoline. On their deck was a sectional couch with a table in the middle. He had decorated out back as well since it was a nice day and he figured people might want to be outdoors instead of in.

Before the girls went out, he got a giant PAW Patrol picture book that had oversized pictures of the pups. He let each of the girls pick their own picture from the set. He then brought out several cups of water to put at the table so that they could dip and clean their brushes, paper towels, and the entire bin of paints and paint brushes. Once the girls were set up, he made his way back inside.

Riley's mother said to him, "We were all back here shaking out heads saying 'No! Don't let them paint!' You're going to have quite the mess on your hands."

"It's okay, they're having fun," Cary replied. Ally loved being creative, so he probably should have anticipated that question in advance and already be setup. But the kids were all painting now.

A few left the paint table and split up. Some on the trampoline, some in the sandbox, and some on the swing set. Then they all gravitated back together again.

"Lunch time!" Cary called from the porch doorway.

The kids rushed inside and took their plates and went along the kitchen counter either taking food or having their parents help them pick out some food. They then made their way over to the kitchen table and all ate, very quietly. Cary snapped a few pictures to make sure he captured the girls throughout the day with whatever it was that they were doing.

After the kids finished eating they went to go play again. Cary joined the Dance School parents on the couch on the porch and they all began discussing the dress rehearsal and the recital. The three mothers all offered to help Cary with Ally if he was not allowed back to help her change for each number. He was so relieved to hear that, and knew Ally would be happy too, knowing that it was the people here today that were helping her.

They made their way back inside the house to open presents, and all of the girls were anxious for Ally to open theirs next. She got games, and arts and crafts, and books, and clothes, and some toys, and a new doll. She was thrilled with it all.

When it was time for the cake, the girls all went into the dining room this time, switching tables on their own. They all sang Happy Birthday to Ally, she blew out her candles, and then they all dug in. Each girl picked whether they wanted a piece of the birthday cake or the corresponding cupcakes. Some even had a taste of each!

After desert, they made their way back upstairs and to

the master bedroom where they asked if they could all watch a movie. Cary came up to check on them and all seven girls were on the bed, surrounded by every pillow in the house, and watching the movie together.

The day soon came to a close, with the girls all saying that they would see each other at Dance School next week. They had one class left on Wednesday, then the Dress Rehearsal on Friday, and then the Recital on Saturday. It was a great day, so much fun, so many smiles, so many laughs, and Ally was the star of it all. He was so glad, so relieved that her friends had come and that everyone had such a wonderful time.

Happy Birthday, Ally! Daddy loves you!

CHAPTER

16

The night before a dance recital is so many things all at once. Fun. Exciting. Anticipation. Nerve wracking. Chaotic. It's a blend of all of the above as the teachers and studio work hard to keep all of the dancers organized and the routines somewhat on schedule. Each class sits together in rows so that when it is their time to get ready—typically three dances before they are scheduled to be on—the entire class gets up as one, walks to the back of the auditorium, and is lead to the dressing rooms in the back.

Every dancer came dressed in their first outfit. For Ally, that was her black penguin tuxedo outfit for tap. It helped keep things moving more quickly the night of and with fewer costume changes. For the actual recital, the kids would come dressed normally, and then switch into each outfit—though tights, makeup, and hair would all be done at home before arriving.

When the kids left the theatre, so too did the parents. Or at least the parent who was helping their child get ready. For the dress rehearsal, since they were told when to get up and go, there wasn't as much of a need to focus on the timing. But for the actual show, it was up to the parent to know when it was time to get up and go and make sure their little dancer was where they needed to be. After all, now the kids were all together; tomorrow they would all be sitting throughout the theatre with their families.

Cary was glad that at the dress rehearsal that nobody objected to him being in the back to help Ally get ready. Not only did she insist that she wanted him there, he felt bad asking the other mothers to help out when they had their own kids that they were responsible for. But even at the dress rehearsal, the kids and their parents who were at Ally's birthday party all stuck together, and the parents all promised to help Ally the following day.

Cary had everything fully prepared to make things as easy and efficient as possible both for the dress rehearsal and for the actual recital. The hanging suitcase they were using had big pockets on the outside. In each sleeve was Ally's shoes, one for each dance. In another big pocket had her hair things—gel, spray, brush, comb, toothbrush, hair-net, pins, and elastics—and in the last pocket he had her makeup kit—with each shade of lipstick that Ally needed, one for each dance, plus her blush, eye shadow, and mas-cara. Inside the bag itself were three hangers, each with a clear plastic bag over it to keep the outfits together—one for each outfit, hanging up so as not to get wrinkled, and one for the finale where she would wear shorts, shoes, and the tshirt custom made for all of the students showing the show and the dance studio. He also had another bag hanging with a pair of extra tights just in case the ones Ally was wearing got a snap or tore and she needed a quick replace-ment.

To help the other parents the following day, Cary showed them where everything was to help make it easier for them. Lyla's mother said, "You're so good at this. So organized."

Riley, Chloe, and Zoey's mother quickly agreed.

The actual dances on dress rehearsal night went very quickly. The emphasis was on placement for the kids to make sure they knew where they began each dance on stage rather than in the studio. But more importantly was the behind the scenes activities of getting ready and being in the right place at the right time. They moved very quickly through the dances, only pausing a handful of times if there was something that the instructors caught that they wanted to fix prior to the show.

For Cary though, this was amazing. Not only could he get to finally see Ally dance—since the classes are behind closed doors—but he could also get right up to the stage when she was dancing and take amazing pictures of her on stage and dancing. Even some video. Announcements had been made in the beginning that it was okay to do that to-night, but not the following day. So all parents should get pictures out of the way at the dress rehearsal.

As soon as the first dance was done, all of the parents made their way out of the auditorium and practically ran through the halls to meet their children and help change them from one outfit to the next.

Cary met Ally in the dressing room and by their bag. They carefully took off the first outfit and placed each item on the hanger and then with the clear bag over it so that it would be ready for tomorrow. He then got the second out-fit—the lime green one—out of its bag and helped her get dressed.

Once they were done they started to head back to the auditorium to watch the other dances before it was time to come back again. They saw Kaitlyn in the hall and the two girls ran to each other, Kaitlyn yelling, "Ally! Ally! Ally!" and Ally yelling, "Kaitlyn! Kaitlyn! Kaitlyn!" Cary took a few pictures of the two and then told them that they should all head back so that they could see what was happening.

With everything moving so quickly, it wasn't long before it was time to head back again. Cary and Ally and all of her friends made their way back to the dressing rooms again. When a stagehand told them to follow her, the parents all waited until their kids, who had lined up, were escorted out of the room. Then they all went quickly back to the theatre to make certain that they did not miss anything.

Once again Cary got up close and was able to take amazing pictures and some video of Ally dancing. The number finished and the girls all left the stage. The parents made their way back again, making the final wardrobe change for the evening.

Like with the first outfit, Cary very carefully put the second outfit back on the hanger, under the clear bag, and then back into the suitcase. The original outfit was on top to be ready for the actual recital. The second outfit was behind it, and when they got home Cary would repack the final outfit and hang it behind the other two.

By the time the girls were in their final outfits, they were allowed to sit anywhere they wanted. All of the girls from Ally's birthday party—Kaitlyn, Rley, Chloe, Zoey, Lyla, and

Tanya—all sat together on the floor in what Ally called "Criss-Cross-Apple-Sauce" style. It was nice seeing them all together. Cary got in front of them and snapped a few pictures for Ally's memories book.

When all of the dances were done, every dancer from throughout the night went up on stage. This one they had to do a couple of times before they figured out the spacing and got it right. Every class would go up one at a time, from older kids down to the youngest, take their bows and get their applause from the crowd, and then go sit, kneel, or stand depending on where they were. By the time the last group came out, everyone was on stage together.

"Okay everybody, that's a wrap. Tomorrow we do it for real."

Cary headed back to the dressing room and waited for Ally along with the other parents. She and Kaitlyn came running in together.

"Did you see us? Did you see us? That was so much fun!"

"And tomorrow you get to do it before a crowd," Cary said.

"Yay!" Ally replied.

"Nervous?"

Ally scrunched her nose and gave him a look that said, "Why would I be nervous?"

"Good girl," he said, giving her a big hug and kissing her on the forehead. He took the suitcase to bring it home for the night. "Ready?"

"Uh huh," she replied.

"See you all tomorrow," he said. "Thank you again for offering to help."

"Oh, no problem," Riley and the twins mother said.

"Glad to help," Kaitlyn's mother added.

"Well thank you nonetheless."

They headed back to their car and then straight home. Cary had Ally change out of her final outfit and then got that arranged and in the bag for the following day. He looked at the clock. It was getting late.

"Do you want a bath tonight or tomorrow before we go?" he asked.

"Tomorrow," she said.

"Okay. Let me just use the makeup remover then so you're not sleeping in it." He carefully removed her makeup, and then asked, "Are you hungry again?"

Ally's eyes lit up. "Can we have ice cream?"

"Oh-kay, twist my arm why don't you," he said, dragging out the "okay" teasingly. "But then right to bed, okay?"

She dragged out her "Okay" just as much as he had, trying to sound like her Daddy.

"Should we do chocolate or chocolate marshmallow tonight?"

"Chocolate," Ally said. "No, wait, chocolate marshmallow."

"You got it." Cary scooped the ice cream and added the chocolate syrup for each of them.

"Can I do the jimmies?" Ally asked.

"Absolutely," Cary said.

"Turn around, it's a surprise," Ally said.

"Ooh, I love surprises," Cary said.

She made a mixture of chocolate jimmies and the colored jimmies and put them on each of their sundaes. "You can look now."

"Magnificent!" Cary said after looking. "You do great work."

"Thanks," she said.

Since it was the night before the dance recital, they decided to watch an episode of World of Dance while they ate their ice creams. Cary let Ally fall asleep watching. She had a big day tomorrow.

N   N   N

And tomorrow came very quickly! Cary made a nice healthy breakfast for Ally, then had her hop in the tub for her bath. Going to the theatre, he had her in her tights, hair, and makeup for the first dance, but normal clothes over it. Cary had a massive bouquet of flowers that he had been trying to hide from Ally until afterwards, but he didn't intend to leave her to sneak them in, and, she would be sitting with him in the audience when she was not dancing.

"Pretend you don't see these," he said as he got them out of the trunk.

"See what?" Ally asked, playing along. But he could tell by how wide her eyes got that she was really excited about her flowers.

When they got there they went straight for the dressing room where there was a guard this time telling him he couldn't go back. He looked inside though and saw Lyla's mother and asked Ally to go get her. She ran right in and the two came back.

"Hi, I can't go in. Can you take Ally's bag?"

"Of course," she said.

"Thank you so much."

Cary then stood there by the entrance waiting for Ally to be done getting dressed. While waiting he thought back to their last recital and the fire and silently prayed that there was no need for Boston or Little Bluey to have to make a cameo at this one. Before long, Ally, Lyla, and Lyla's mother all came out together.

"Thank you again."

"My pleasure."

Ally and Lyla hugged each other and then stood next to each other so that Lyla's mother and Cary could get a picture of them. Then they all went to find their seats until it was time to go back again. Cary and Ally were on the righthand side of the theatre, whereas Lyla and her mother went to the left.

When they got in, they spotted Riley, the twins, and their mother sitting in the very front row in the middle section. They did not see Kaitlyn and her parents, but they had to be here somewhere.

Unlike the night before, most of the lights went off and one of the Dance School instructors kicked things off by thanking everyone who came and talking about all of the hard work and dedication that the dancers had put into it all year long. Then she left the stage and the first group of performers came on.

Cary followed along in the program book, making sure that he got Ally up and back when they were supposed to go. He saw Riley and her mother get up a dance earlier than he expected and walk quickly to the back between numbers and whispered to Ally, "Looks like its time."

"Yay!" Ally said.

By the time they got to the back of the theatre, the doors were closed again and they had to wait until that routine was done. Unlike he and Ally who had been at a different

Dance School before this one, Riley had been in this one before. Knowing that the doors would be locked during the performances must have been why they got up a dance earlier than they needed to. But as soon as the dance ended the doors opened and they made their way out.

Cary brought Ally back, and again had to stop at the door. He told her to go in and to find Riley's Mom. She did so and he waited there until Riley's Mom came out, signifying that it was time to go back to the theatre.

"Thank you for helping her out."

"No problem. I'll help her get changed after this dance, too."

"Great, thanks, I appreciate it," Cary said.

He got back to his seat and after one dance, it was Ally's turn. She came onto stage and waved at him when she got to her spot. He waved back. Then the music came on for "Flip Flap." The girls began waddling like penguins, wiggling, then pointing, then clapping, bouncing up and down, and then tapping. There were eleven girls on the stage for the performance. Riley was right in front, smiling wide and leading the rest of the class. Lyla was right behind her in the middle. Ally was three dancers to the left, staying right on beat with the rest of the class. Kaitlyn was on the right hand side, two kids away from the middle. They were all so adorable and Cary could not keep a smile off of his face as he proudly watched his daughter dancing.

"Flip Flap goes the beat. Flip Flap goes the beat. All right penguins..."

He hardly even heard the lyrics as he could only focus on his daughter. Then it was over and she gave a big bow before she and the rest of the girls made their way off stage. Cary got up at once and saw Riley's mother already rushing for the doors. This time he made it through and back to the dressing room door where he waited for Ally.

Riley's mother helped her with the costume change and then Ally came running out to him and leapt into his arms.

"Daddy! Daddy! Daddy! Did you see me? Did you see me?"

"I did!" he said, smiling. "You were amazing. So adorable."

Ally didn't want to go back to the theatre right away. She wanted to see her friends. So she, Riley, Kaitlyn, and Lyla all stayed and chatted for a bit. When it was time for Chloe, Zoey, and Tanya to take the stage, the girls were ready to go inside to watch.

When they were four dances from Ally's next routine, they headed back again and got her ready for her next dance. Just like last time, Cary waited for Riley's mom to come back out so he knew Ally was in and all set, and then returned to his seat.

The second number, her jazz dance, was to the music of "Move Your Feet" from the movie Trolls. This dance had more dancers, seventeen on stage, with Riley still in front directing the class and Lyla right behind her. Ally was still on the left side and Kaitlyn on the right. This time they began crouching down, and when the music came on and Poppy said, "Everybody, move your hair and feel united," all the girls came up as one, raised their arms and began shaking them in the air. This dance had more movement, more steps, more waving of arms, more jumping around, and more leg kicks built into the choreography. At one point they lay down, heads up and their legs kicking. Then they got back up and resumed dancing again. At the end they all took their bow and exited the stage. Just like before, Cary could not stop smiling.

Cary rushed back again and waited for Ally to be done changing and come out. "That was fantastic!" he said. "You were great!"

Ally's smile widened from ear to ear. "Thanks."

"Should we go watch the rest?"

"Yeah," she said.

There were fifty-four performances in all before the grand finale. Cary brought Ally back for the finale and then made his way back to his seat. The finale though was very different than it had been the night before. Instead of the dancers all walking onto the stage and bowing, they actually danced to the music of "I just want to celebrate." It began with older dancers, then the curtains opened and even

149

more dancers were on blocks dancing n the background. Then more and more dancers kept coming out to join the dance, with the newer dancers moving to the front and the ones that had been there moving to the back. There were so many dancers that several songs played for the entire finale as the students kept on with the performance, all wearing white shorts, their matching tshirts, and with bare feet.

Ally's group came marching out, their lime green bows still in their hair. They all bounced up and down, fist pumping in the air with the beat, spun around, bounced some more, spun around again, jogged in place and then headed back as the next group came up.

It was great seeing the finale number, so much more than just the kids walking in and bowing. He wondered when they all worked on it since they did not rehearse it the night before. But it all worked out perfectly. A great ending to a great performance. Majestic.

An announcer spoke over the speaker system and said, "We would like to thank you all for coming and hope you enjoyed Celebrate the Music. We look forward to seeing you all again next season."

Cary headed back to the dressing room and this time there was no guard blocking him from going in since none of the girls would be changing anymore. Cary went in and found Ally talking with her friends as they all excitedly spoke about the recital and how it went. When she saw him, she can rushing over.

"I'm so proud of you," he said as he very formally presented her with her flowers. "These are for you, my lady."

"Oh Daddy, they're beautiful."

He never was one to accept floral arrangements as they were. He would putter and pick things out, sometimes merging multiple bouquets of similar colors to bring out what he really wanted. It was quite the bouquet that she had.

As she ran over to show her friends her flowers, Cary retrieved her suitcase and made sure everything was back in there where it belonged. He thanked Lyla and Riley's mothers again for all of their help throughout the day. He didn't know how he would have managed without them there.

After some more time with friends, it was time to start heading out. The other girls were taking pictures with their siblings, parents, and grandparents. Ally looked sad for a moment.

"What is it, honey?" Cary asked.

"I wish Grandma had been here to see me dance."

"Me too," Cary said. "Me too." After a silent pause, he said, "How about we go out to dinner to celebrate?"

"Yeah!" Ally shouted.

"I know just the place," Cary said.

CHAPTER 17

While Ally and her Daddy were out celebrating after a successful dance recital, Sign and Signah were being dropped off at their home by the ambulance. It had been a long road for them, from the hospital to a rehab facility, but now they were being brought home to resume their lives. The only question was whether it would be as Sign and Signah, brother and sister, or as Bad Guyie and Crystal, super villains.

"Bring them this way," their mother said, opening the door for the ambulance driver. Normally the kids would have been picked up at the hospital, but because of Sign's condition the ambulance brought him home and were making sure that they could get him inside all right. A visiting nurses firm would then follow up and make sure both kids were okay and transitioning back to normal and arrange for their continued health and any physical therapy that they still needed.

The two paramedics brought Sign in and set him in his new motorized chair. They looked around, judgmentally in Signah's opinion, but did not say anything other than, "Good luck," before leaving.

Ever since their transformation, Signah felt like she was doing fine. It was Sign who was having the most trouble with his lost limbs. People looked at them differently now. Treated them differently. She hated it.

"Well, welcome home," their mother said. "You know where everything is. I have to go to work."

"Yeah, sure," Signah said. "I'll take care of everything." As usual.

After their mother left, Signah sat down next to her brother.

He looked over at her. "Can I do it now?"

Signed nodded approvingly.

Sign closed his eyes and concentrated. Rocks and stone came snaking their way toward him until they touched his body. He then was able to use them to form limbs and stood up out of his electric wheel chair.

"Ah, that feels so much better. I missed this."

"I can imagine," Signah said, twirling her crystal between her thumb and forefinger. "You know, we're home now. We haven't seen that crazy doctor again. We don't have to do anything."

Sign pondered that for a moment and then shook his head. "I'm not angry anymore. I'm not. But a deal's a deal. Doctor-lady could come back and take our powers away. You wouldn't want that, would you?"

"No," Crystal admitted. Life was so much easier, so much better before the storm. They never had the best homelife, but things certainly were better than this.

"Then we're agreed?" Sign asked.

"We're agreed," Signah replied.

The rocks fully covered Sign's body and face. When he spoke again it was with the booming voice of Bad Guyie, "THEN LITTLE BLUEY'S DAYS ARE NUMBERED!"

CHAPTER 18

The end of the recital marked the end of their scheduled activities. Ally hadn't had her real birthday yet, but she had her party and her recital. This was the time of year when school-aged children would be getting out for summer break. It also marked the final few months before Ally would need to begin going to school.

For her final summer before school, Cary wanted to make sure that Ally had a memorable season. He began exploring options of things that they could do, from swimming to camping to the Museum of Science to the Aquarium to a ballgame to amusement parks. Heidi recommended someplace called Storyland, which she said would be perfect for Ally. A nice little road trip for a day or so to get away.

The summer was also a good opportunity to try and have some playdates with Ally's friends from Dance School. Just because the recital was over and they didn't have classes again until September didn't mean she had to miss her friends. Everyone was a phone call, text, instant message, or email away.

While Cary was contemplating what activities he could plan out, Nanny hovered in.

"Are you ready to review my findings?"

Cary had to think for a moment. "Findings for what?"

"My research into other potentially enhanced individuals," Nanny reminded him.

It had been a while since his encounter with the two super powered individuals. The research project had definitely been put on the back burner, but would still be good to know. "What did you find?"

"More than you would think," Nanny replied. "It was our initial hypothesis that this world did not have individuals with abilities. That enhanced individuals, or those with special gifts, did not exist. However, that was not the case."

"So there are people like us?" Cary asked.

"Probability matches for inexplicable sightings, scientific

experiments, technological leaps, arcane and supernatural phenomena, and documented specimens of evolutionary traits."

"Sounds like you found a lot," Cary said.

"It has taken me some time to cross reference and corroborate my findings," Nanny said, her robotic voice sounding smug.

"Is the origin of Bad Guyie in your findings?"

"Negative."

Cary was tempted to say "Keep digging," but knew Nanny would never be able to stop even if she could not find anything. Instead he said, "Well done. Create file entries for each individual with a corresponding probability for an actual ability. If we ever need it one day, it might be helpful to have a directory of potential allies or threats."

"Compliance," Nanny said.

Ally stepped into the doorway of his office and said, "Daddy, are you done?"

"Do you want the park, Museum of Science, or Aquarium first?" he asked.

"All three!" Ally said.

Cary chuckled. "One at a time. We'll get them all in. Do you want to do one today?"

As Ally was thinking about it, Nanny interrupted them, saying, "Pardon the intrusion, but a child swam too far

157

from shore and is floundering."

There were undoubtedly life guards on duty, but this was a good mission for Little Bluey to swoop in and save the day. They had been so busy of late that they hadn't done much superheroing.

"Want to suit up?" Cary asked.

Ally's eyes lit up as she activated her necklace and her suit flowed over her. "Ready!"

Cary shuffled his hands through her hair. "Always prepared. I love you." He got into his costume too, and said, "Let's go save that child."

Their lair brought them to an underground tunnel. Time was of the essence with a child drowning, so Cary had Ally hold onto his neck and he leapt down the tunnel. The tunnel ended with an entrance in the woods so that they could come and go without anyone easily identifying which house was theirs or zeroing in on their location. Once they were out of the tunnel, Cary leapt into the air, Ally still holding on tight, and soared through the sky. The lake was two leaps away, and they made it in record time, landing on the sand of the beach and seeing people standing around and pointing out at the water where arms were floundering in the water.

"Remember, for someone drowning, do not just try to grab them. They may pull you down," Cary cautioned. He then looked around and saw a buoy hanging on the life-guard's station. "There, use that. Throw it down to them and pull them up or have them hold on and drag them back to shore."

"Okay," Ally said, flying over to retrieve the buoy and then out over the water.

Cary watched, carefully monitoring the situation. He could not fly or walk on water, but if Ally needed him, he could leap out and be within feet of the floundering child to try and help out.

She was half way to the child when the sand began moving up his legs and then wrapped around him. "What the...?" Before he could finish his thought, he lost his footing and struck the ground. He struggled, but it was sand holding him and more kept coming and holding him down. He looked around, trying to find the source of his problem, and then he saw a familiar figure walking toward him.

↗ ↗ ↗

Little Bluey soared over the water, the ring of the life buoy in her hands. She got to the floundering child and tried to sound reassuring.

"I'm Little Bluey and I'm here to rescue you."

She saw just arms splashing in the water and realized

that the child had no way of hearing or understanding her. She still tried again.

"Here, grab this and I'll pull you to safety."

She dropped the buoy down, holding the end of the rope that was attached to it. The frantic arms floundering brushed against it, and then clung to it for dear life. Little Bluey could see the child more clearly now, a little boy who looked to be about her age.

"Hold on, I'm going to bring you in to safety," she said. The boy nodded. She then turned to fly back to shore, expecting to see her Daddy standing there and watching her, but instead she saw him floundering in the sand just as this boy had been doing. "Daddy?"

There was no answer over their comms. Her Daddy needed her. She began flying fast, dragging the little boy along with her. It was almost like he was water skiing or tubing they were going so fast. But her Daddy needed her. He was in trouble, too, and she needed to get there to rescue him.

⚡ ⚡ ⚡

"YOU CAN'T SAVE HER THIS TIME!" Bad Guyie shouted. His focus was on Boston Bluey and keeping the hero down. But he dared a glance out over the water and saw Little Bluey soaring right toward him. "HERE SHE COMES!"

"I see her," Crystal said. She touched her crystal and activated her powers, absorbing the magic inside of her. "There's something I want to test out."

She then waved her arms and an aura or purple light cascaded from her fingertips and engulfed nearby items. A first aid kit by the lifeguard station opened up, gauze rolled out and then bonded together to form a creature that looked like a mummy. A bottle of suntan lotion began to ooze out and rose from the ground like a creamy blob. A crab was struck and grew in size to be as big as a car, its claws snapping as it pranced along the beach. The fire from one of the grills in the camp area burst forth and took shape into a flaming behemoth.

"Rise my minions, rise!" Crystal shouted. "Look upon our enemy and keep her away from Boston Bluey!"

The newly formed monsters obeyed their master and made their way between Boston Bluey and the shoreline where Little Bluey was soaring in at them.

"SHE HAS NO CHANCE, NOW. NEITHER OF THEM DO!"

N N N

Even through the sand Boston Bluey could hear that booming voice clearly. It was Bad Guyie. No matter how hard he struggled to free himself, tried to move, kicked his legs to leap in the air, the sand kept holding him down. But there was another power he had. One that he had often used to enhance his strikes more than unleash in its primal fury. But this was the time to cut loose. This was the time to show just what he could do, and what an impact that could have on things like sand.

Lightning, if the conditions were right, could strike sand, especially sand on a beach, if the temperature of the strike makes it hot enough and the sand has a high content of silica or quartz, could fuse the sand into glass. The lightning strike blasts through the ground, creating hollow, glass-lined tubes with a sandy exterior, or, in other words, it could make petrified lightning. It was quite magnificent, and something he had never tried himself. He also did not emit lightning bolts, but could emit electrical currents. He would have to channel it intensely enough to make the sand hot enough to super charge and transform to glass. But Little Bluey was counting on him. He had to do it.

He stopped moving, stopped resisting, instead focusing on his innate abilities, and summoned it as best he could. Then when he could feel the charge surging through his body, he released it, his fingers, his hands, his entire body bursting forth with electrical current. He hoped that none of the beachgoers were too close by and could be impacted, but this was his last, best hope. He kept forcing the charge until he felt his body becoming depleted. Was it enough?

Around him he heard crinkling, as if the sand were turning hard and into glass. Then he heard a scream. A loud, booming, rock-like scream.

"AHHHHH!!!!!! WHAT IS HE DOING TO ME?"

Then Boston Bluey tried to move again, tried to propel himself upwards. This time he felt glass shattering as he leapt up from the ground and landed off several feet from where he had been. He felt weak, woozy from both his expended power and not being able to breathe for a few minutes, but he was free.

⚡ ⚡ ⚡

Little Bluey flew over to the shore and yanked the rope upwards so that the child she was towing could carry on to the beach with the momentum. Her first task in saving the child was done. Now she had to save her Daddy.

She felt relieved when she heard Bad Guyie scream and then saw her Daddy burst from the ground. But then the quartet of creatures blocked her path, keeping her from him. It was like something out of a nightmare with monsters preventing her from getting to her Daddy.

But he was okay she could see, and she was a superhero. It was time to act like one. She looked at the monsters keeping her from her Daddy. A gauze mummy, a suntan blob, a giant crab, and a fire creature. Her Daddy had always taught her to keep her wits about her, to not give in to the pressure or dire nature of a particular situation, and try to find a solution. What was her solution here? How could she beat these creatures?

She reached to her belt and drew a metallic rod that with a flick of her wrist opened up to be the bow she had made. She could only fly. She needed something more to deal with these monsters. But would a bow and arrows even hurt them.

Little Bluey nocked her first arrow and released it. The arrow sailed harmlessly through the suntan blob. It took a tittle of the lotion with it, but the arrow had gone right through.

"That didn't work," she said to herself. Before she could think of something else, a stream of fire lanced out at her from the fire creature. Little Bluey dodged and swooped out of the way, right into the reach of the giant crab, who began snapping at her. There was no break in sight. She had to figure out something.

✦ ✦ ✦

Crystal watched as her minions were dealing with Little Bluey. The superhero had tried unsuccessfully to attack them. She would not be able to defeat the mystical minions. Even if they had a weakness, Crystal doubted very much that a little girl like Little Bluey had any hope of figuring it out.

But this fight wasn't only against Little Bluey. She shifted her attention to Boston Bluey. Whatever he did, turning the sand to glass, had hurt Bad Guyie. It was up to her to save her brother.

"We haven't been properly introduced," she said. "The name is Crystal, and you should give up now or see just what I can really do."

✦ ✦ ✦

Boston Bluey struggled to catch his breath, gasping for air. It was like sweet tea to him right now, quenching his thirst. The girl with Bad Guyie, Crystal, was walking toward him, threatening him. So far he knew she could send beams of power like in their first encounter, open portals, and now apparently bring things to life to serve her bidding. What else could she do? How was she doing this? And how could she be focused on him and the creatures she created still be fighting Little Bluey without her attention?

"You said you'd leave Little Bluey alone if I gave up?" he asked, trying to distract her.

Behind Crystal, Bad Guyie had stood up and seemed to have recovered. "HER FATE IS SEALED. BUT WE ONLY WANT HER."

"No deal," Boston Bluey said as he leaped forward and delivered a massive Earth-shattering punch to Bad Guyie's face. Unlike their first encounter, Bad Guyie did not intercept him this time. He must have been taken by surprise.

Bad Guyie flew several feet off of the ground and up into the air. The rocks and stones flowed off of him and Boston Bluey could see what looked like a handicapped little boy. As the boy landed on the ground, he hit hard and lay there, the stones and rocks not pulling back to him.

"Sign!" Crystal shouted.

"I'm sorry," Boston Bluey said. "I didn't know he was a little boy."

Crystal turned on him, her eyes ablaze. The paint upon her face contorting into an evil demonic mask. She then reached for her crystal and said, "You'll pay for that."

N   N   N

Little Bluey flew back out over the water. She had an idea. Water douses flames. Maybe she could figure out a way to put the fire creature out and eliminate one of the threats. It was the crab though that came out into the lake after her.

She flew up high, dodging again as another stream of fire lanced out at her. She then knew what to do. She began her dive into a barrel roll, heading straight down for the water by the edge of the beach closest to the fire creature. She knew she had to time this perfectly. She could see the giant crab closing in. The fire creature taking aim. At the last second she pulled up, just as the crab pounced and the fire creature emitted another burst of flames. The crab landed hard, causing water to splash and hit the fire creature. The flames hit the crab and sent it squealing and out deeper into the lake.

Little Bluey flew up high and hovered, clapping her hands triumphantly when she saw that the fire creature was gone, only wet sand and some steam smoking where it had been, and the giant crab was swimming away.

She did the math real quick, proud of herself for knowing this, and said, "Two down, two to go."

Taking her attention away from the last two monsters, she glanced around from her bird's eye view to try and find her Daddy. She saw him standing several feet from the purple and black garbed girl. There was no sign of Bad Guyie. But she did see a poor defenseless little boy laying near the fight. He had no arms and no legs and would clearly get hurt as an innocent bystander. She couldn't believe that his Mommy or Daddy had run away when the fight began and left him behind.

"I'll save you," she said. She then soared down, just as the suntan blob tried to grab her with it's lotion-arms. She easily dodged the advance and made it to the boy. "I'll save you," she said again.

She was not as strong as her Daddy, not super strong at all, actually, but this little boy needed her help. She put her arms around his body, gently lifted his head from the ground, and then with all of her might flew straight up in the air just as the gauze mummy tried to ensnare her.

"I did it!" she shouted excitedly.

◢ ◢ ◢

"I did it!"

The shout woke him back up. Sign was disoriented at first, but then realized that he was flying with Little Bluey. In the air, he could not summon the rocks and stones and become Bad Guyie. He had to physically be touching the ground for his powers to work. He was totally at her mercy.

"What are you doing?" he demanded.

"I'm saving you," Little Bluey said matter-of-factly.

"You... are saving... me?" Sign asked, feeling confused.

"Of course. That's what heroes do," she said, and ended it with a reassuring smile. "I know you can't hold on, but I got you."

"You got me," he said. All of the anger, all of the resentment, all of the bile that had been plaguing him since the storm when he had not been saved just flowed right out of him. Instead he felt a renewed sense of innocence and warmth. She had saved him after all.

Little Bluey was still looking at him, then turned her head to the side. "You look awfully familiar to me."

"You do too," he said back, then laughed.

Little Bluey laughed, too. She then flew down to a landing near where the people who had been at the beach were waiting. "You should be far enough from the fight here." She gently set him down and then took back to the sky. "Take care."

Sign watched her go, then said to himself, "She saved me." He then said it again, louder this time, "She saved me! Little Bluey saved me!" Without even realizing what he was doing, merely wanting to reach out for her, now that he was touching the ground, rocks and stones flowed to his body and encased him again. "SHE SAVED ME! ME!"

✂ ✂ ✂

Boston Bluey felt horrible that Bad Guyie turned out to be a kid. He looked like he was about Ally's age. That giant rock creature with the booming voice and fists that could hurt even him was just a child. He had hurt a child. That thought, the memory of the punch, kept cycling through his mind and was eating away at him.

"You'll pay for that! I'll make sure you pay!"

Crystal was coming right for him, crackling with energy. Was she just a child, too? He had to be careful. He had to stop them, but not risk hurting them. The suntan blob and gauze mummy moved to flank him so he had to fight all three. There was no sign of Little Bluey or the other two monsters.

Boston Bluey spoke into his communicator. "Where are you?"

"Coming back to you now," came the reply.

Crystal touched her necklace again and the two monsters attacked.

"Go for the necklace," he instructed. "The one Crystal is wearing around her neck. I think it's the source of her power."

He leapt up into the air to escape the suntan blob, but his legs got tangled by the gauze monster and was dragged back down. For a creature made of medical tape and gauze, the mummy was stronger than it looked. As soon as he was on the ground, the suntan blob was atop of him, and for the second time today he couldn't breathe.

※ ※ ※

"Go for the necklace. The one Crystal is wearing around her neck. I think it's the source of her power."

Little Bluey flew back overhead and scanned what was going on below. Her Daddy was in trouble again with the two monsters. She had to save him. She reached for her bow again and then flew to make sure she was at the right vantage point. She nocked an arrow, aimed, prayed that she had done enough target practice, and let the arrow go.

※ ※ ※

"That's it! Kill him! Kill him for what he's done!" Crystal shouted, her eyes still ablaze as she glared at the gurgling Boston Bluey, trapped within the body of her suntan blob monster. Then something whizzed by, brushing her chin, stinging, and in an instant her connection to the creatures and her magic was lost. "What?"

She glanced up and saw Little Bluey, holding a bow,

looking down at her. She turned and looked down and saw her necklace laying on the ground, the chain broken, an arrow wedged in the pavement. She then looked over at Boston Bluey and watched as the suntan blob lost it's cohesion and just became normal lotion again. The gauze mummy unraveled and blew away in the wind like a kite.

"No!" she shouted, reaching for her crystal.

"Don't do it!" Little Bluey shouted from above.

Boston Bluey stepped closer, trying to sound reassuring. "It's over. There's no need for harm."

Then she heard her salvation storming toward her.

"WAIT!"

All heads turned to see Bad Guyie charging at them.

N N N

"Little Bluey, take to the skies!" Boston Bluey ordered so that she would get out of harms way. He wished he could make sure Crystal stayed away from her necklace, but Bad Guyie was too powerful of an enemy. He may just be a boy, but his punches hurt, bad. He had to be careful.

"WAIT!" Bad Guyie shouted again.

Crystal retrieved her necklace and the purple aura began flowing around her again. Boston Bluey glanced back and forth. This was not over yet. But then something peculiar happened.

"WAIT!" Bad Guyie shouted again, reaching Crystal and coming to a stop. The rocks in front of his face fell off revealing the face of the boy below, and also returned his voice to normal. "Everyone just wait."

Little Bluey flew over to her Daddy and landed. "You're the boy I saved."

Boston Bluey looked down at her and then over at their enemies. "You saved him?"

"He was lying by the battle. I brought him to safety." She then looked at Bad Guyie. "You're the bad guy? Why do you want to hurt me?"

"I don't," the boy said. "I'm sorry I ever did. It was all a misunderstanding."

Crystal was as shocked as anyone. "Are you sure?"

"She saved me," Bad Guyie said. "She really saved me."

"That's all you ever wanted," Crystal said. She let her crystal go, holding onto the broken necklace and letting the crystal dangle.

"He's not a bad guy after all," Little Bluey said. "He's a good guy."

Bad Guyie laughed and said, "I like that. Bad Guyie no more. Now, you can call me," the rocks flowed back over his face and his voice became booming again, "GOOD GUYIE!"

"Good Guyie or not, a lot happened here. There's going to be questions. People are going to demand answers," Boston Bluey said.

"Maybe one day we can make amends," Crystal said. "I'm sorry we attacked you both. A tale for another time." She then flicked the crystal into her palm, activated her power, and a portal opened beneath she and her brother.

Before they vanished through the portal, Good Guyie said, "WE'LL BE SEEING YOU, HEROES." And then they were both gone.

Boston Bluey reached over and pulled Little Bluey to him, holding her tight and hugging her. "Are you okay?"

"I'm okay," she said. Then added sadly, "They were keeping me from you. Are you okay?"

"Knowing you're okay, I'm doing great," Boston Bluey said. "Really great."

CHAPTER 19

"This is Evie Berman, WTB TV, reporting live where moments ago there was a superhero battle between Boston Bluey, Little Bluey, Bad Guyie, and Crystal. We are here with Boston and Little Bluey. Could you tell us what happened here?"

"We came to the beach to respond to the report of a child that was drowning. Little Bluey saved the boy and returned him safely to shore," Boston Bluey explained.

"Very admirable," Evie Berman said. "But what about the battle against the super villains?"

"There were no super villains," Boston Bluey said. "It

was a couple of kids using special effects and trying to gain their fifteen minutes of fame."

"Can you tell us who these kids are?"

"Let me just say that Little Bluey and I came to an understanding with these kids, and they will not be bothering anyone again. They are not super villains that the people have to worry about."

Little Bluey then added, "And it's not Bad Guyie, but Good Guyie!"

Signah turned off the television.

"Why did you do that?" Sign asked. "They were talking about us."

"I don't want it to go to your head," Signah said, teasing him.

"Do you think we'll ever see them again? Little Bluey and Boston Bluey, I mean."

Signah nodded silently as she twirled her crystal. "Real soon."

Sign thought about her answer and then smiled. "I'd like that."

✕ ✕ ✕

"Were these really supervillains, or kids playing a prank? Either way, authorities should keep an eye out. This is Evie Berman, WTB TV News. Back to you, Greg."

Cary watched the entire broadcast and wondered if he had helped diffuse the situation or if Good Guyie and Crystal would have problems with the law. Was the authorities on this world even equipped to handle super powered individuals? Unless they brought the military in, a gross overreaction, he doubted it.

The thought of the military becoming involved worried him. Here were a couple of kids who didn't know any better. How many other kids were there in the world with abilities that could get them into trouble? Fear, paranoia, mistrust of things that were different than you. That seemed to be a multiversal language. But what could he do to fix that? Short of hiding all of the kids away that had abilities, finding some secret new home or safe haven for them he, didn't know what he could do.

"Nanny, let me see those files."

"Compliance."

The files projected before him, displaying images of the people. He could touch the image and more elaborate records opened up based on Nanny's research. He reviewed a dozen files before Ally woke up from her nap. He stopped his work instantly, intrigued by what he had seen, and vowing to go back and look at it some more. He had a lot of reading to do, a lot of thinking to do, and decisions to make. But not tonight. Tonight he was going to spend time with his daughter and love every minute of it.

"Happy Birthday, honey," he said.

Ally clapped her hands excitedly. "I'm five now!"

"Yeah you are," he said, giving her a hug. "You're growing up so fast."

"Not fast enough," Ally said.

"Too fast," Cary replied.

EPILOGUE

The wind started to gust, out of nowhere lightning began to strike, and a loud crackling noise could be heard for miles around. Then a hole tore open in the very fabric of space, and something came through. Something not of this Earth. Something new coming here from someplace else.

On their hands and knees, it was a person, a woman. She slowly lifted her head up to scan her surroundings. Everything was foreign. So different from where she had come from and what she was used to. She spotted vegetation. Growth. She crawled over to it, and brushed it lightly with her fingers. A newly formed flower was growing close to where she was.

"Well that's good." Things were not so different here after all. Grass still grew. Flowers still bloomed.

She reached up and touched the temples of her head, trying to concentrate, trying to feel for what she was searching. "I am looking for people," she said to no one at all. "I have traveled far. This world is strange to me," she looked up to the nighttime sky and failed to recognize any of these constellations. "This world would be strange to them, too. People with powers, not like mine, but powers."

She looked around, scanning her surroundings again. "I was promised that this would work. That this would bring me to them. A man and a little girl. My visions are never wrong." She closed her eyes, trying to visualize them, and then searched for nearby minds that may be aware of them. Finding thoughts, images, she felt a surge of hope. "You will be my eyes and ears. You will help me find them."

There were more thoughts as she reached further out. More people who might be able to help her. "With you, I will find the ones I am looking for."

The woman slowly stood up, feeling what the gravity on this planet was like, and then began walking toward the source of the most thoughts—where she would undoubtedly find the most people who could help her. She was patient, and she was determined. She would find them. She knew she would. It was only a matter of time before she located Ally and Cary Archer.

Boston and Little Bluey will Return !

For more details and information,
visit www.SilverLeafBooks.com

Audrey's Artist Alley

Overview: Every book will have the artists front cover, but Audrey will also take the raw black and white images and color them herself, demonstrating her own artistic development over time as the series continues.

Painted: 4/27/19

Artist Insight:

With the original Boston Bluey cover, Audrey opted to use Glitter Gel pens. For the sequel, she has been more in the mood for painting.

She began with Little Bluey and used "Violet Flicker," a glittery shade of purple. For her legs and mask, she used traditional pink, with an aqua blue for her boots. She used yellow for both her skin and hair, with a red hair tie.

Boston Bluey is predominantly a shiny blue paint, with the same pink and violet flicker used on Little Bluey to finish the outfit. His hair is brown, and his eyes blue.

New character Bad Guyie, she began with his rock arm and used grey. She then made his costume with both traditional yellow and red paints, with brown for his hair.

New character Crystal, she went with violet flicker for her outfit, a light purple for her hair, and pink for her leggings and shoes.

For the background, she used foam stars and flowers, painted them yellow, and stamped the background to make clouds. She then let the painting dry overnight. In the morning she completed the sky with a glittery-blue, and then the grass with a glittery-green paint.

ABOUT THE AUTHORS

CLIFFORD B. BOWYER is the creator and author of The Imperium Saga universe. *Boston Bluey* is his first collaboration with his daughter. Bowyer graduated from Bryant College with a degree in both Management and Marketing, and received his MBA from Babson College. Bowyer continues working on developing future installments of his novels. He resides in Massachusetts with his daughter, where he coaches and plays softball, and launched a superhero toy company in honor of Boston Bluey with his daughter, ACB Toys & Collectibles. Visit us at: www.ACBToysCollectibles.com.

AUDREY BOWYER at her young age has always had a thirst for learning and a desire to know how to do things. She loves using her imagination, being creative, exploring, going on adventures, dancing, horseback riding, and playing. When she suggested collaborating on *Boston Bluey* with her novelist Daddy, she immersed herself in the story and really helped bring the characters to life. She excitedly continues to create new ideas for future challenges that will face Boston and Little Bluey.